The Black Horse

and Other Stories

By the same author

Poetry
Country Road and Other Poems 1953
The Turning Wheel 1961
Experiment in Form booklet, 1964
Day Book: Poems of a Year 1966
Shadow Show 1968
Song for a Guitar and Other Songs 1976
Walking on the Snow 1976
Steps of the Sun 1979
Collected Poems 1987

Other
Sawmilling Yesterday 1958
Curved Horizon, an Autobiography 1991

Children's Fiction
The Children in the Bush 1969
Ragamuffin Scarecrow 1969
A Dog Called Wig 1970
The Wild Boy in the Bush 1971
The Big Flood in the Bush 1972
The House on the Cliffs 1975
Shining Rivers 1979
Holiday Time in the Bush 1983

The Black Horse
and Other Stories

Ruth Dallas

University of Otago Press

Published by University of Otago Press
56 Union Street/ PO Box 56 Dunedin, New Zealand
email: university.press@stonebow.otago.ac.nz

First published 2000
Copyright © Ruth Dallas 2000
ISBN 1 877133 85 X

Five of these stories have appeared in *Landfall*:
'The Letter' (1961), 'Lily of a Day' (1962), 'The Visitor' (1970),
'The Black Horse' (1978), 'The Macrocarpa Hedge' (1980)

Published with the assistance of
Creative New Zealand

ARTS COUNCIL OF NEW ZEALAND *TOI AOTEAROA*

Cover image by Kathryn Madill
Printed by PrintLink Ltd, Wellington

Contents

Stewart's Farm

In the afternoon, Snowy Stewart, a farmer from Burnt Valley, wearing his navy-blue suit, which now stretched tightly over his bent shoulders, returned slowly to his faded blue truck, which he had parked in a surburban street in Invercargill that morning. He had parked his truck in the suburbs so that he could walk the rest of the way into town and look more closely at the houses that lined the streets and which had never before attracted his attention.

On earlier trips all he had noticed was that they seemed built so close together he wondered how people could live on such small patches of ground. Lately he had felt his strength was failing and that he should consider moving to town, and his doctor, whom he had visited that morning, had encouraged a move. But walking back to the truck he no longer looked at the houses.

He did not want to move from the farm, which was the only home and workplace he had ever known, and where his father worked before him, breaking in the land, felling, burning and draining. He himself was still dynamiting the stumps of the old burnt bush, and that job was not going to be finished in his lifetime.

He dumped into the tray of the truck his bag containing some replacement parts for his milking machine, and climbed into the cab, but did not immediately drive off, though it was already mid-afternoon and he needed to be home for the evening milking. He sat thinking with renewed regret of the loss of his son, Murray, and of all that had been lost when he was killed in the war. He should have been here to continue with the work and would have inherited a valuable property to pass to sons of his own. The farm would not always be remote. There was talk about improving the road and taking it through to the bush that was still waiting to be cleared. Although it was the last farm, it could be the first if that area of bush was cleared and settled and the electricity brought in.

Murray had known well enough that work on the farm was classified 'essential' in wartime, and that he was under no obligation to join the armed forces, but he enlisted with his cobber, Danny Murphy, the only son of the storekeeper, who had been killed, too. There was no store at Sandywell since then. When Mike Murphy couldn't find a buyer, he'd simply closed down and moved to Nelson with his wife Peg. Their daughter, Kathleen, had already left home and gone up north. Murray used to be sweet on Kathleen. What was the point in giving up the store? You just have to carry on. He had stayed on the farm with Sarah. But Mike did not care about his store as he, a farmer, cared about his farm.

It was after Murray went overseas that the Manpower Board sent out that unfit farm-worker, Tom Archer, as a replacement, and unfit he certainly was. Fit only to play dance music on Sarah's piano. That was when he was milking thirty or forty head, and half the time the bugger was so dreamy he tried to let the cows out without untying the leg rope. Whenever there was work to be done, Archer was ill. Sarah had liked him all right.

Returning to thoughts of Sarah, he felt his heart beat fast. What was her idea in taking the deeds of the farm and borrowing money on them, as he had discovered only this afternoon from his lawyer, in the firm that had been his father's, where he had gone to talk about selling the property. Sarah had gone to a strange solicitor and never paid the money back, only the interest, all these years since the war. What could have happened that she was so secretive? Surely it had nothing to do with Tom Archer? Could that whinger have got the money out of her? He would face her with it and see what she had to say. It was hot in the cab. He took off his jacket, rolled up his shirt sleeves and drove home.

The farm was down a side road that ended at his gate, a mere grassy track with dark green fields on either side where his beef cattle grazed among clumps of reeds and where an occasional stack of old tree stumps was piled to dry. The home paddocks were clean pasture surrounded by gorse hedges. The farmhouse was already in the shade of the macrocarpa belt planted years ago, a solitary low white weatherboard cottage with a corrugated iron roof painted red, built by his father and looking very comfortably settled among the outbuildings. How could he ever have thought of leaving, he wondered.

He was late. Sarah had opened the gate for the cows and they were gathered at the shed and in the bails, only fourteen black and whites where once he had milked thirty odd, but enough to bring a cheque from the cheese factory. Sarah did not help with the milking. He saw her moving back to the house, walking stiffly, with a slight limp, as she was troubled by rheumatism. Once she had been straight as a fence-post, a tall strong woman with black hair, now turned grey. Entering the house, he had no time to talk, nor did he want the tea and scones prepared for him. He passed into the bedroom, glad to change from his town clothes into dungarees and gumboots.

He did not get back to the house till it was too dark to continue working on the milking machine, fitting the replacement parts he had brought from town. It was an old-fashioned petrol-driven machine that he couldn't replace without bringing electricity on to the farm, which he considered an unnecessary expense. He managed very well without it.

Sarah had lit the lamp in the kitchen and kept his meal hot in the oven, but he pushed his plate aside half-eaten, saying, 'I had a good meal at a pub in town. A cup of tea is all I need.'

He watched her with puzzled interest as she moved about the room from the coal range to table and bench in her customary unhurried manner. She was ten years younger than he was and always looked calm and resigned. She had been a good worker, but now moved more slowly. He first met her when she came to the Sandywell Hall to play an accompaniment on the piano for another girl, and when he married her she brought her own piano with her from Tuatapere. It still stood in the front room, where she played on it from time to time. He remembered that she played for Iris Jenkins at the farewell concert in the hall, for the boys of the district when they were home on final leave. There were five boys, including Murray and Danny Murphy, standing up on stage in their khaki uniforms, red-faced, embarrassed while they listened to speeches. Iris Jenkins had sung *Oh Danny Boy the pipes the pipes are calling* ... Peg Murphy was upset. Sarah took it quietly, but later hung a photo of Murray on the kitchen wall.

'What did the doctor say?' she asked as she set his tea on the table.

'More pills,' he said. 'I left them in the truck.' Then after stirring his tea for a while, he said, 'I've been thinking of moving to town.'

She looked at him in disbelief. 'Leave the farm? You will never leave the farm.'

'I've been thinking about it,' he said.

'Oh, yes?' She continued to look at him with a wry smile. 'You've often said you won't leave till you are carried off.

The farm is everything to you.'

'Dad left his papers in the drawer of the dresser in the front room. Are they still there?'

'As far as I know,' she said lightly, turning her back and working at the bench.

He felt his heart hammer in his chest. He hardly knew how to begin. He looked around the room, which was just the same as it had always been, the same kitchen table where his mother had baked and given him the spoon and bowl to lick, the same clock on the mantelpiece which his father once took to pieces and put together again and which he still wound every Sunday night, the same black stove with its wire rack and brass rail for airing clothes. Nothing had changed, yet everything now seemed stale.

'I was looking for the deeds of the farm,' he said. 'Dad left them in that drawer. I looked for them and couldn't find them. I went to the lawyer to see if he knew where they were. Do you know where they are?'

Sarah turned and stared at him. Then sat slowly on the edge of a kitchen chair, drying her hands on a towel.

'A nice thing!' he said in his most sarcastic voice. 'A wife borrows money on her husband's property behind his back for reasons unknown. What was the money for?'

'Please don't ask me that.' Her face turned scarlet. She laid aside the towel and pressed her cheeks with the knuckles of both hands.

'I shall find out.' He waited a moment. 'You went to a crooked lawyer, not Dad's firm. The man had no right to lend you the money. You haven't paid it back. You've paid the interest all these years. I can't understand it.'

'I couldn't tell you at the time,' Sarah said, 'and I can't tell you now.'

'Did Archer get the money out of you?'

She stared at him in amazement. 'Tom Archer? What

could he have to do with it?'

For a long time there was silence between them.

'Tom Archer was always a sore spot with you,' she said at last, in her old resigned scarcely audible voice, not looking at him, and with a helpless gesture with her hands. 'But there was nothing in it. You couldn't understand why I tried to help him. He was a poor fellow who needed help. It's just your own mad possessive way that puts ideas into your head.'

'You must have wanted the money for some reason,' he said. 'Why couldn't you open up?'

'What was the use? All our years together you've kept the money. You tell me I get my living off the farm, but you don't know what it's like to have no money to use in your own way, to have to ask for every little thing and then to be refused, though it might only be a tap inside the house that you wanted when you're weary of carrying in water and carrying it out again. What was good enough for your mother was good enough for me. The money I borrowed – and I wish to God I could have got it paid back – had nothing to do with Tom Archer. It was for Murray.'

'Murray knew about it?' He looked up at the framed photo of Murray in his khaki uniform as though expecting him to protest.

'People could be hurt,' she said.

'What people? Who?'

'You, for one. And Murray. And Kathleen Murphy. And Peg and Mike and Danny Murphy.'

'What on earth – ?'

'I don't suppose it matters now,' she went on in the same low voice. 'Peg and Mike went to Nelson after the boys were killed. Murray wanted the money to send Kathleen to Christchurch for an abortion.'

'Kathleen had an abortion?'

'That was the intention. But she took a job there and was

transferred to Auckland and the baby was born in Auckland, a boy. As far as I know she's still there. The child was adopted from birth. Peg and Mike didn't know. No one knew. Murray made me promise. He had no money. You wouldn't give him a wage, though you had to pay Tom Archer a wage, when Murray had gone. You used to say he would get the farm some day. When you were done with it yourself, I suppose. But the day has come and gone for Murray, and there was nothing he had from the farm, for all his labour. It was after that trouble he enlisted and went away. And he needn't have gone. He would have served the country better on the farm. Now he's dead!'

He saw her turn and bury her face in her arms on the back of her chair in the abandonment of grief, as she had done when the news came that her son was killed.

But he was not able to put his arms around her now.

'A grandson –' he muttered. 'To carry on the farm – adopted out!'

Walter's Mother

Walter's mother propped her son's postcard against the vase of roses and, sinking heavily on her creaking wooden chair, rested her arms on the table. Although she had read his words a dozen times, the brightly coloured card still seemed to entice her like an unopened parcel. Sharon would see it there as soon as she came home for lunch. But what could be delaying Sharon today, of all days? Through the kitchen window she could see the leaves of the sycamore tree next door turning back in the wind, but the sky was blue and without cloud and the sun had shone all morning after yesterday's rain. She had opened the windows in Walter's room, washed his curtains and swept the wallpaper with a broom, but now her arms ached.

And after all, when Sharon came in, red-faced and hot from biking against the wind, she read the card only once and turned it over, giving more attention to the coloured view of Auckland on the other side.

'Home Saturday night by train?' she said, seating herself at the table. 'Tomorrow night? I was going to bowls. Why does he leave it till the last minute – and why doesn't he write a proper letter?'

They sat in silence, each occupied with her own thoughts, the mother dismissing Sharon's unanswerable questions and wondering what Walter meant by 'short trip', when he was coming so far, while Sharon fell into an old pattern of brooding resentment, remembering that he had gone north and left her with the care of her mother and the large garden with its hedges and lawns.

'There's a horrible wind blowing,' she said. 'It stopped me at the corner and I had to get off my bike.' She sat hunched over the table as though the wind still blew against her, that unmanageable lock of dark hair falling over her forehead as usual. Was it biking against the wind that made Sharon round shouldered at thirty, or was it bending over her desk in an office all day? It was better for her to come home and have dinner at midday as her father had done.

A door banged shut in the passage and startled them.

'That's Walter's room,' the mother said. 'I left the window open to air it. I've dusted it, but there's dust on the wallpaper that I can't reach – I can't raise my arms as I used to. Some time tomorrow would you – ?'

Without looking up from her plate, Sharon said, 'If you want to spring-clean his room you should let me take down those old swimming certificates – yellow and fly-spotted. They've been up since he was at school.'

'They will stay on the wall. I was so proud –' Why did Sharon have to bring up that old argument now, of all times? What could she know of a mother's pride?

'Everything in the room is exactly as he left it, as though he had died. Nothing has been changed in three years. But Walter has changed.'

No, your children didn't really change. When they were little you could see their personalities forming and they remained essentially the same throughout their lives. Walter was an affectionate child and would always be affectionate. Sharon had been hard to love, she was such an independent little Miss.

'As long as I am alive Walter's room will be kept for him just as it is. He's working in Auckland now, but one day he will come back to Invercargill. This is his home as well as ours.'

16

'Then I wish he would stick around and help with the garden.' Sharon, looked around the room as though seeking escape. 'I can't keep up a quarter-acre on my own. If this is his house as well as ours, why doesn't he help? How are we to get it painted? The roof leaks and the spouting is broken. Nothing has been done since Dad died. Meet the train – spring-clean his room – taking it for granted we will be here to receive him. If I had gone north and he had stayed, would he spring-clean my room?'

'I don't know what he means by "short trip",' the mother said, beginning to clear the table and stack the dishes hurriedly because she intended to go to town as soon as Sharon had gone back to work. She would not tell Sharon she was going to buy a new hat for the occasion. They were back in fashion again and she had seen some nice ones in church lately.

Walter's old girlfriend, Lynn Fletcher, was the first to see her new hat, in the bus on the way home. When Lynn looked into the plastic bag and saw that soft pink hat decorated with net her eyes grew round with surprise.

'Will Walter come to church with you on Sunday?' she asked.

There was a time when the mother thought Walter and Lynn … and such a lovely girl, with the Fletcher red hair. All the girls in that family, even generations back, were fine-looking girls. Lynn had cried when she came to the station to see Walter off on the train.

'Walter wouldn't forget old friends,' she told her. 'You must come and see him again.'

Lynn blushed and looked out of the window, saying, 'He will have a girl in Auckland now.'

Getting down from the bus and turning to wave to Lynn, she suddenly felt extraordinarily agitated and was seized by such a sharp pain in her chest that she could hardly remain standing. She looked for somewhere to sit down and considered the gutter, but knew she would not be able to get up again from such a low position. Although the wind pressed against her, she struggled to keep walking and reached a paling fence where she could steady herself. Resting there she felt a little better and noticed that the wind had strewn broken branches along the footpath. The wind had spoilt a bright sunny day.

At home she put one of her prescription pills under her tongue to ease the pain and lay on the sofa thinking with satisfaction of her hat. In the mirror in the shop it made her look so much younger, concealing her white hair, and very suitable for the occasion, the saleswoman had said.

She was still resting on the sofa when she saw Sharon pass the window as she wheeled her bike to the shed. The fire in the stove had to be built up to fry the fresh blue cod she had brought from town, so she stood up and straightened the cushions so that Sharon would not know that she had been lying down. To surprise her, she put on the hat.

'You've been to town in this wind?' Sharon could hardly believe it. 'This is just to meet Walter? But the doctor said you were to rest at home quietly.'

'Do you think it suits me?'

'It's not what I think that matters – it's what Walter will think,' Sharon said bitterly. 'I hope he won't think it's something to eat.'

That was just to tease her. She pretended to be offended and went back to her room and put the hat in its bag. She would never tell Sharon how much it had cost – more than Arnie would bring home in his pay packet when they were first married, and quite shameful.

Of course it had to rain the next day, all day, with water shooting from the broken gutters and that old leak staining the wallpaper in Sharon's room. Then, at the very last moment, just before the taxi came to take them to the station, Sharon came into her room and found her with the hat on and declared she ought not to wear it.

'It will get wet and be ruined!' Sharon's eyes flashed angrily from under the red hood of the raincoat she wore to work.

The mother felt confused. Sharon was right. Her hands shook as she fastened her coat.

Sharon, noticing her agitation, said 'You shouldn't be going out at all on a night like this. You could wait at home.'

'Of course I must meet the train.' She looked defiantly at Sharon. 'And I am wearing it.'

Then the taxi came and they were hurried off to the station, where they found a place to sit on one of the long wooden seats that were like the seats in the public gardens, except that they had an advertisement on the back saying 'Go to Ferguson and Watkins first'. There were not many people at the station. The lights showed wild gusts of rain sweeping across the tracks.

'For Walter – anything –' Sharon said, shivering, and sinking deeper into her red hood.

'Do you remember the time you went to Timaru with us in the train? Uncle Fred and Effie were living up there and we had a holiday with them. But they didn't settle and came south again. Why didn't we go further when your father was alive? I haven't been to Christchurch. It's all day in the train.'

Then she heard the whistle sound unexpectedly near, and standing up hastily, almost lost her balance. The carriages were rolling by too fast for her to see Walter at any of the windows. When they stopped she could see nothing but the sides of the train streaming with dirt and rain. Sharon was shaking her arm and saying, 'Here he is!' and he was standing quite close, taller than she remembered, and with a black beard!

He kissed her and said, 'I've got a surprise for you,' tipping up his head in that mischievous way that she knew so well that it brought tears to her eyes. 'I've brought Tracy.'

Sharon nudged her. 'He's brought a girl!'

'We're married,' Walter said. He drew forward a girl who was wearing ornamental glinting glasses that half-concealed her face so that it was difficult to see what she was like, especially as she had an abundance of thick black curly hair that reached to her shoulders. She was a big girl and wore a loose unfastened black-and-white checked jacket.

She kissed the girl's cheek and managed to murmur, 'My dear –' before the tears filled her eyes and everything was blurred.

'Not waterworks,' Walter said, laughing and putting his arm around her.

'We have to grab a taxi.' Sharon hurried them along. 'This rain –'

'Back to the sunny South,' Walter said.

To be married and to say nothing about it! That was the hard part. Their voices swirled around her in the taxi and she could not understand what they were saying.

Sharon had the key for the front door and they took their bags to Walter's room. Alone in the kitchen, the mother glanced anxiously over the table set with her best cloth and the forget-me-not teaset that Arnie had bought for her one time after he had been drinking. Absently she brought another cup and saucer from the china cabinet and polished them with a tea-towel. As she removed the damp cloth from the plate of ham sandwiches made with mustard for Walter, though neither she nor Sharon liked mustard, she wondered whether Tracy liked it. His favourite chocolate sponge had risen well and looked nice on a gold-edged plate. She poked up the fire and moved the kettle over the flame.

Walter and Tracy came into the room with their arms

around each other, with Walter saying at once, 'You've had the kitchen papered.'

'I wrote and told you about it – a terrible businesss – the walls had to be stripped and we had to get the ceiling done as well – and the man charged more than he quoted – I wrote and told you.'

'I don't remember.' He ran his hand over the new paper. She drew a chair to the table and asked Tracy to make herself at home.

'I wanted Wally to let you know we were getting married,' Tracy said, with an embarrassed laugh. She had taken off her jacket and was wearing a black pullover and black trousers. She was pregnant – quite stout. She looked unfamiliar, not at all like Lynn or any of the Fletcher girls – a big dark girl with an easy air of assurance. The pair brought a smell of cigarette smoke into the room.

'I wanted to surprise you,' Walter said. 'We're going on to Queenstown on Wednesday. Tracy's never been in the South Island.'

When Sharon came in she said, 'You've still got on your hat and coat, Mother.' Then, turning to Walter, 'How do you like Mother's hat? She bought it specially to meet the train.'

'It's a knock-out!' Walter laughed, and Sharon, too. They laughed teasingly and affectionately, but their remarks hurt. Something hurt. She didn't quite know what it was. She felt the young people had joined forces against her.

Going up to her room she noticed they had left the light on in Walter's room and that Tracy's checked jacket lay on his bed. How strange it was to see it lying there! And Walter looked different. It wasn't only the beard, but something else as well. He had a guarded look. She could hear their voices.

'The old girl's showing her age,' Walter said.

Then Sharon's voice, 'The doctor says –'

Was that what they called her? 'The old girl!'

She removed her hat in her room and looked to see whether any rain had fallen on it, brushing off a few damp spots with her handkerchief. She felt protective towards it, as though it, too, had suffered disappointment. 'They will be old themselves one day,' she said, addressing the hat. 'Their children will grow up and get married and not think about them.'

Her face in the mirror surprised her, revealing such a deep red colour, like the colour of anger, an old woman's face, her white hair flattened. She picked up her comb. The rain was still beating on the roof and tumbling from the broken gutters to the ground. It was cold here. But it would be warm in the kitchen. She smiled, forgetting the mirror, combing her hair, and remembering that Walter was home.

The Letter

Rain had been falling for some days. Sheets of water covered the low-lying paddocks where the farm was not yet drained. Black stumps, the only remnants of the burnt bush, still poked from the land like broken and decayed teeth. A pile of uprooted stumps and blackened branches had been stacked beside the milking shed, which was an old closed building, like a barn. This shed and the square brown farmhouse nearby were the only buildings visible in the lonely, half-cleared countryside. In the shelter of the wood-pile stood an outdoor copper, like a large insect. A feeble thread of smoke trailed from the copper chimney, unable to rise in the damp air. A woman, huddled under an oilskin, crouched before the fire-box, trying to coax the fire to burn and the water to boil. It was eight o'clock in the morning, the milking was nearly over, and the water that would soon be needed for scalding the milking machines was still only lukewarm. Presently the woman went to the door of the shed, where her husband was milking in the half-darkness inside. The last half-dozen cows were in the bail.

'Owen! If I only had –' Her voice faltered, she seemed close to tears. She made an effort to shout above the noise of the machines, and her voice rose shrilly. 'If I could just get a little dry wood!'

Her husband came out and began to dismantle the wood-pile with his strong hands. His movements were active, quick, rather impatient. His jersey, woollen cap, trousers, were mottled with rain, his gumboots coated with wet mud. The woman was slow, large, heavy, and in her husband's great oilskin seemed like a dark tent. When he had shifted a few stumps the wood in the centre of the pile showed up, dry and dusty. His wife bent forward to pull out a log. 'Just a minute, Brenda, there's some smaller stuff underneath.' He heaved aside a heavy log and his wife stooped and gathered some dry chips and roots that had long ago been twisted and dried by the sun.

'It's all right in fine weather,' she said. 'In rain like this – I can't help it – I think about the McDonalds' electric heating.'

'They have to pay for the electricity,' Owen said quickly. 'They don't get it for nothing. They haven't got the wood we've got.' He ducked back into the shed.

The woman cut the wood with the heavy axe and fed it into the fire-box. Smoke billowed freely from the tin chimney and lingered over the yard. She went to a corner of the shed and looked across a green paddock towards the house, where she had left her three children. The square wooden house was brown in the rain, its red roof gleaming wetly. Behind it the bush stood black and drenched, brooding and withdrawn. The chimney of the house was without smoke; she did not light a fire in the house till the milking was finished, she had to leave the children alone. She had left Susan and Judy safe and warm in her big bed and the baby asleep in his cot. No face showed at the uncurtained window. As though satisfied with what she saw, she turned and went into the shed.

'I could make you a bit of a shelter,' Owen said. His voice came muffled, his head in its woollen hat was pressed against a cow's side as he sat stripping. 'I've got those kerosene tins. Flatten them. Put in a post or two. Join it onto the end of the shed.'

'It's just the rain,' the woman said.

When the milking was over and she had finished her work at the shed, she threw the oilskin roughly over her head and shoulders, took up a bucket of milk for the house, and picked her way steadily over the wet paddock.

As she drew near the house she could hear the baby awake and crying. She tugged off her gumboots at the back door, hung the oilskin on a nail, and as soon as she opened the door, the two little girls threw themselves upon her with a glad release of energy. They were still in their pyjamas and carried their clothes in their arms. 'Dress me! Dress me!' demanded the younger. 'Judy broke Ronald's truck!' cried the elder. "Waah! Waah! Waah!' sounded from the cot. The house seemed full of live hungry creatures, like a bird's nest. The woman sighed with relief as she set the bucket of milk on the bench. She had been down at the shed for two hours.

'One at a time,' she said. She brought the baby out to the kitchen, soothed him, gave him a crust of bread to chew and stood him in his play-pen, which Owen had made from a large packing case. She lit the fire, put the porridge on to boil, dressed the smaller girl and helped Susan with her clothes. Susan was four. All this she did quietly and quickly, yet without hurry, as she did everything about the house and shed. She was heavily built, dark-skinned, not handsome, but strong and steady, with beautiful still brown eyes.

Owen came in for breakfast and said no more about the shelter. But all morning, after he had gone down to the shed, she heard the sound of hammering on tin. As she moved about the house, washing dishes, making beds, washing the children's clothes, preparing dinner, the muffled clang-clang came to her above the roar of rain on the iron roof over her head.

'What's Daddy doing?' Susan wanted to know.

'Opening out kerosene tins. Making a shelter for the copper.'

'I want to go and see.'

'No, stay here in the warm kitchen with Judy and Ronald. You can go out tomorrow when it's fine.'

Susan knelt at the window, on a chair, watching the rain. The glass was clouded with steam from the pots on the range; she rubbed it clear with the palms of her hands. She could see the road and the flooded paddocks but, today, she could not see the far-off hills. 'Here's the mailman,' she announced presently. 'Stopping at our gate.'

Her mother moved to the window. Letters came so seldom to the farm that this year the birds had built a nest in the mailbox and she had left it there for the children. Only last week she had pulled out the old straw.

'Daddy will get the letter,' Susan said, as the mail-car pulled away.

Bang! Bang! Bang! rose from the shed.

'He hasn't seen,' the mother said.

'Can I go and get it?'

'No, Daddy will bring it later. It's nothing.'

'I'll go and tell Daddy.'

'Stay here, out of the rain.'

She cooked the dinner, fed the children, and still the hammering came from the shed. At last she dressed Susan in coat and gumboots and a sou'wester and sent her out to call her father.

From the window, with the baby in her arms, and shielding Judy so that she would not fall from the chair, she watched him take the letter from the mailbox and stand staring at it as though he had forgotten the rain. There's something wrong, she thought. She waited at the window, watching as he came up to the house, Susan following like a calf at his heels.

The shuffle at the door, gumboots, coat, Susan's gumboots.

'What is it?'

His face was wet, he brushed the water away with his sleeve.

'A letter from Bert, I think.' Her feeling of uneasiness increased. The last letter they had received from Owen's brother, Bert, years ago, had told of the death of another brother, Vernon. When someone died you sat down and wrote a letter and told the others. For what other reason would you write?

He took the letter from his pocket.

'Haven't you opened it yet?'

'You don't hear from Bert very often.' He examined the envelope suspiciously. He almost seemed to doubt that it was for him. He opened it and stood reading by the window.

'What's he mean?' he asked sharply, looking up. 'Sheep! I can't run sheep. I've got to think of the mortgage. There's no quick money in sheep. You have to wait.' He passed her the letter and retained a slip of paper in his hand. The letter was written in a childish scrawl on half a page torn from a notebook.

Dear Owen
Hows the old bush farm coming along you want to get the cows off of that place and get onto sheep I made good money out of sheep. If I was to tell you how well I got on you would not believe it you would reckon it was all me eye and Betty Martin. I am sending you something to help along. I am yours truly Bert.

'It looks like he sent a cheque,' Owen said. 'Five hundred pounds.'

The woman sat down suddenly on one of the kitchen chairs and let the baby slide gently to the floor. 'Let me see!'

'It's not proper. Look! It says "Not Negotiable".'

'What's that mean?'

'What do you think it means? It means it's not negotiable.'

'What's negotiable mean?'

'You know what negotiable means!'

'How do I know what it means? Let me see!'

He handed her the cheque. 'Not negotiable!' she read aloud, wonderingly.

'That's what I say. How can it be cashed if it's not negotiable? Who would take it? A man would only make a fool of himself. I haven't got much faith in Bert.'

'He seems to have done well.'

'All skite.' He took the cheque and put it with the letter back into the envelope, and tucked it behind the clock on the mantelpiece.

'Your dinner's spoiling,' the woman said. She whipped hot plates for herself and Owen from the oven to the table.

Owen ate his dinner absently. He looked round the room with its shabby wallpaper, soiled by the children's hands, the worn linoleum, the black range, the scrubbed kitchen chairs, the linoleum-covered table. He could spend five hundred pounds over and over again. If the cheque was good he would not know what to do first. A few sheep? An electric water-heater for the shed? Better cows? Wallpaper for the kitchen? No, no – the mortgage came first. If he could just get a bit more paid off the farm – He pushed his plate away, his dinner unfinished. 'What a dirty trick!' he said.

'He mightn't 'a done it on purpose.'

'Bone? Bone?' cried the baby, pulling himself up against his father's knee.

'Give Ronald your bone,' the mother said.

But he did not hear. 'A rotten dirty trick!' he said.

'It might be all right,' the mother said.

The baby began to wail. 'Bo-one! Bo-one! Bo-one!'

The father stiffened. 'Shut him up!' he cried abruptly.

She picked the baby up, but he would not be soothed. 'Bo-one!' Tears gathered in his eyes and ran down his cheeks. The mother sneaked the bone from his father's plate and gave it to him. She sat at the table, nursing the baby, wiping away his tears with her apron. The two little girls sat still on the mat where they had been playing and looked up at their father with saucer eyes.

He sat with his arms along the table, his eyes unseeing. 'One Christmas,' he said, 'I fought with Bert. Mum was in hospital. Bert was the eldest and he was in charge of us – Vernon and me. To pay me out he took Vernon to a friend's place for Christmas dinner and he didn't take me. I was only a kid.'

'What did you have?'

'Nothing. What do you suppose I had? Just what I could find in the cupboard. You don't forget that sort of thing.' His face flushed darkly.

He rose and took the letter from the mantelpiece and looked at the cheque again. With a movement of impatience, he suddenly crushed it and dropped it into the fire. 'That makes an end of it,' he said, and he went out, slamming the door roughly behind him.

'Horrid letter,' Susan said, scowling.

'Daddy burned it,' Judy said. She drew near to her mother and looked into her face. Her round dark eyes sought for confirmation. 'Daddy burned it, didn't he, Mummy?'

'All gone,' the mother said. She sat motionless, puzzled. Judy, satisfied, returned to her play.

The baby began to poke the bone into his mother's mouth. She roused herself and pretended to bite it, snapping her strong white teeth. The baby began to laugh, to roll and gurgle with laughter. He held the bone out to Judy and Susan. They must bite too. As they tried to bite, he pulled the bone away, giggling, rolling, helpless with laughter. His laughter was infectious; they all laughed – the baby, Susan, Judy and the mother. The kitchen was filled with the sound of their laughter. It drowned the drumming of the rain.

Lily of a Day

Some people become absorbed in whatever they are doing at the moment, as though nothing else existed: they write letters in a crowded room, they remain calm when other people are in tears; in the midst of confusion they seem unperturbed as a lily on a pond. Linda Foster was like that. Even at fourteen, with her heart-shaped face, her high cheek bones and narrow grey eyes, her soft composed mouth, she had the mask-like features, the air of tranquillity, that was to be hers for all time. She wanted to be a nurse; she found that she would have to wait till she was eighteen, but she didn't mind, she said.

That year, when Linda was fourteen and I was ten, Linda's mother had rented a holiday crib down the harbour, and took me along to keep Linda company. The crib stood on a high cliff above the water, dwarfed to a doll's house by a row of tall blue-gums that grew along the cliff's edge. Beyond the blue-gums there was nothing but sky and water. We had come from flat town streets, and the feeling of height and space enchanted us. Between the blue-gums and the crib lay a pleasant field of untrampled flowering grass with only a narrow footpath winding across it. But on the first day all was still half-hidden by rain.

Linda sat in the window-seat with her head bent over her sewing as though her stitches were of the gravest importance, not looking up at the gusts of rain streaming down the glass, or the blue-gums waving wildly outside in the wind. I sat at the table, idly cutting out scraps from some old magazines I had found. The sighing and hissing of the blue-gums came through the open fanlight, disturbing me. I wanted to be outside, but the rain fell in sheets. I kept watching Linda, fascinated by her absorption in her work. All that day, our first day, the rain fell, the blue-gums tossed without rest, and we stayed inside. The roof leaked, and Mrs Foster had placed basins and buckets on the floor to catch the rain; ping, ping, ping, the drops fell steadily into the enamel washing-up basin by the leg of the table. To keep us entertained she made toffee, stretchy, soft, unsuccessful toffee, which stuck to its enamel plate. Towards evening, when the rain showed no sign of easing, she wrapped her legs in brown paper and string, like two parcels, donned an enormous mackintosh that hung behind the door, and set off to walk to the store, which was about a mile away.

Linda and I were left alone in the dark, well-worn living room, which smelt of its own smoky chimney and the kerosene in a lamp that stood on a dresser. Everything seemed gloomy and unfamiliar, and I couldn't shake off the feeling that we had no right to be there. The previous tenant, a woman, had been drowned in the harbour. Mrs Foster had not thought to conceal this from us, accustomed as she was to Linda's serenity; but I knew at once when I heard it that my own parents would not have told me, and I was haunted by it, wondering if any of the things in the room were hers. That mackintosh that Mrs Foster had taken from behind the door, for instance. The rain, the dripping roof, the blue-gums waving wildly as though they were tormented, the being left alone with Linda in the strange room, far from home, unsettled me, and I should have been afraid to stay there if it had not been for Linda's familiar, undisturbed, gentle face, bent over her sewing as though she were in her own home and her stitches were all that mattered in the world.

The light from the window fell upon her work and her bowed head. Her skin was pink and freckled, her lashes fair as though she were red-haired, but her hair was brown, cut short, and curling about her face in an abundant, becoming, womanly fashion. It was hard to believe she was the same age as my cousin, Marion; she seemed so much younger. She had been Marion's friend, at first, not mine; but their interests had grown apart. She was, Marion said, 'too tame', meaning by this that she was not interested in boys. Marion used lipstick and eye-shadow, and practised mysterious glances over her turned-up coat collar. But I didn't find Linda tame. When she showed me her pictures of little Island children, with their hands and feet deformed by leprosy, and pictures of the stiff, white, ghost-like figures who were the nurses who looked after them, and told me with that calm light in her eyes that she longed to go to the Islands and nurse the leper children, I would be filled with admiration and dread.

'But you might get it yourself, Linda!'

'I wouldn't mind,' she would answer dreamily.

Once she showed me a pamphlet about a vegetarian hospital in Australia. 'There they don't eat fish, flesh or fowl,' she said, spreading the pamphlet before me, like a teacher. 'Instead, they eat fruit and nuts.'

At ten years, this diet seemed to me much more interesting than fish, flesh or fowl, and so I stared at the photograph of the large hospital buildings and asked her if she would wait for me and take me nursing with her, if she went there.

'All right,' she said. 'I could wait.'

Then she came to my place on Sunday after bible class with the news that girls in India were married at the age of ten.

'They live in darkness, in India,' she said solemnly. 'They need missionaries and nurses. Terrible famines come to the land. The people die on the roadside.' We fetched the tin globe of the world from an old cupboard, wiped off with our sleeves the grains of borer dust that had fallen on it since it was last used, and traced how far it was from New Zealand to India. 'You could go anywhere, really,' Linda said, running her finger over Egypt, Italy, Spain. 'Nurses are needed everywhere.' So calm was she, so easily did her finger slide over the globe, the world seemed to lie before us like the streets of our own town. We felt we were at the beginning of everything; we could go anywhere. No country was too distant; no language too great a barrier. Where Linda went, I would go, too.

This subject had the added interest of being forbidden. Linda's mother had forbidden her to talk of nursing, and had burned the pamphlets. Linda's father was dead; she was an only child. Her mother feared that nursing would take Linda away from her, and said so openly. Mrs Foster was a lonely, sad little woman, with a tight mouth, and grey hair pulled so tightly back from her face that you could see the shape of her skull beneath the thin flesh, set with prominent, anxious, light grey eyes. I felt she did not like me, or my cousin Marion.

But she had been kind to us that long, wet, first day at the crib, helping us to pass the time indoors, and it was only after she had taken the mackintosh and left for the store that the strangeness of the crib pressed itself upon me.

At last it grew too dark to go on cutting out scraps at the table. I roused myself from a daydream in which Linda and I, in our white uniforms, stood waving from the ship's rail. How sad and strange it seemed to leave my mother and father and brother. Supposing we were drowned? Tears of homesickness came to my eyes. 'Linda, I can't see. How can you go on sewing?'

At once Linda put down her sewing. 'We'll light the lamp,' she said.

Before she could cover the flame with the glass chimney, a little moth blundered into the light and burnt its wings. As it fell to the table she hit it and killed it, at the same moment that I cried out, 'Don't hurt it!'

She smiled at me. 'They only live a day,' she said, and brushed it from the table.

'It's awful to die,' I said. This was something that had troubled me since one of my cousins had been drowned duck-shooting the year before. Now there was the woman who had been drowned in the harbour. Was this her lamp? Was she watching us? I was not used to lamplight and looked uneasily into the dark corners of the room. 'Do you think people that are drowned ever come back?'

'The dead never come back,' Linda said, 'or Daddy would have come.' She turned up the flame and brought her sewing to the table. The friendly light fell upon her work.

Mrs Foster's steps sounded on the patch of gravel outside the door and a moment later she stood in the room with the water streaming from the mackintosh, the brown paper round her legs sodden to a pulp, her shopping bag packed with groceries. She was solid, and human, and had brought us food, and all my fancies at once vanished. Only in sleep they came back to haunt me.

In the morning I woke to the sound of bees outside the window, to the real world, where the rain had ceased. The sun shone, the sky was blue, the tall gums were almost still; sweet air from the harbour sifted through their branches, bringing a feeling of open water beyond. In the grass beside the house countless dandelions, which the day before must have been closed in the rain, had come out like stars. It was a perfect summer morning, with every leaf washed clean.

Linda and I threw on our clothes, and without waiting for breakfast ran slithering and slipping down the wet steep cliff path to the road below, and the open grey-blue harbour water. Then we climbed back up the longer, more sedate gravel road that wound along the cliff top between the houses and the gum trees. As we climbed we tore long lengths of flowering convolvulus from the lupins by the roadside and decorated ourselves hilariously with the white flowers. 'They only live a day,' Linda said, as she wound herself round with their leafy, wreath-like stems that seemed to fall limp almost as soon as plucked.

It was the first time I had seen them. Though some flowers were spoiled by the rain, others were so fresh and white they seemed touched with green, reflecting in their silkiness their own green base and leaves.

'*A lily of a day,*' Linda began to recite in a sing-song, '*Is fairer far in May, Although it fall and die that night* –' and then, as though sensing we were not alone, we both stopped short in the midst of our capers and stared at a girl in a red skirt who stood in a gateway, watching us. The girl stood in a graceful posture, one leg resting on the other, one hand upon one hip. She threw us a mocking glance.

'Small things amuse small minds,' she said, in a superior, grown-up manner.

Linda at once gave a cry of recognition. 'Meg Armstrong! What are you doing here?'

At this I, too, recognised Meg. She was an old playmate of Linda's who had moved to Wellington; but if Linda had not spoken I should not have known her, she was so greatly changed. Her pale hair, which had been straight and flat, had become a mass of dry curls; her lips were reddened; earrings shone in her ears; she wore a white transparent blouse, a red velvet skirt, fine stockings, and red, high-heeled shoes. As we drew near we saw through her blouse the strange narrow shoulder straps and lace trimming of the underwear that grown-ups wore. There was an overpowering smell of scent. In a flash of self-consciousness I saw Linda and myself as I thought Meg saw us, two straight sticks of children, in coarse cotton dresses, bare legs and sandals, festooned with weeds from the roadside.

'Nobody calls me Meg now,' the girl said, with a rabbit-like wriggle of her nose and short upper lip. 'My name is Margaret.'

'What are you doing here?' Linda asked again.

'Same as you, I suppose,' Meg said, lazily. 'Holiday.' She put her hand behind her head and stretched her body languidly, as though with boredom, and looked about her. Then she suddenly stiffened and said, unexpectedly, and with a kind of spiteful hiss, 'In this cemetery!' Her narrow, half-closed eyes that were like the eyes of a cat when they are half-closed, moved unseeingly over the blue-gums, the deserted gravel road, and the half-hidden, silent holiday homes that dozed among the wild grass and overgrown hedges.

The convolvulus wilted in our hands, a shadow, as of a cloud, passed over the grass where the crickets sang, and where a pair of white butterflies chased each other from flower to flower. The stones of the gravel road lay damp and still.

'You're mad!' Linda said, brushing away the bewildering moment as though it were a cobweb. 'It's lovely here.'

'It's dead,' Meg said. 'You should see Wellington! You should see the crowds of people! Did you know I was working? I go up five storeys in a lift every day of my life. I work in an office where there are twenty-five people, all in one big room. We have no end of fun. Fancy coming straight from that to this!' She glared about her angrily.

'Everyone has to have a holiday,' Linda said, staring at Meg as though she wondered if what she said could be true.

Meg changed her tone, became friendly. 'Come for a walk down to the bay,' she said, with a soft, supple, dancing movement of her limbs, 'and I'll tell you something.'

'Can't,' Linda said. 'We haven't had our breakfast. And I have to help Mum with the housework.'

Meg closed her eyes and shuddered. 'I *loathe* housework,' she said.

It seemed to me that an unbridgeable gap would stretch between the two old playmates now, as it had done between Linda and my cousin Marion. Instead, Linda seemed to overlook the change in Meg, as she would have overlooked a pair of crutches, or a rash of pimples; it was something that was there and must be accepted.

'We could come this afternoon,' she said, thoughtfully. 'You come up for us after dinner.'

Mrs Foster let us go, reluctantly, and with many cautions about not losing our way or falling in the water. It was plain to see that she had the feeling she ought not to let us go at all.

The bay offered neither shells nor sand, only sharp and slimy stones. For paddling one needed old shoes, but anyone could see at a glance that Meg was past such a childish amusement as paddling.

A cool afternoon breeze blew off the harbour, ruffling the water, which had changed to a hard bright blue. Its colour suggested a holiday feeling; we strolled along the road not knowing what to do with ourselves. A small dark wharf poked out into deep water and two boys sat fishing from the end. We walked out on the wharf, Meg's high heels making a strange, grown-up tapping on the boards.

I thought at first that Meg must know the boys. As we approached, they rolled their eyes at each other, and one said, 'Look who's coming!' And the other said, 'Look who!' One was a rough-looking boy, with a head of thick short hair like a cap; he wore a khaki shirt and fawn trousers; the other was sleek, like a puppy, with black oiled hair plastered flat on his head; he was white-faced, thin and tall, in a white open-neck shirt and grey flannels. Meg swept them with a glance from beneath her lashes, tossed her head, and strolled about in a bored fashion, not looking at them.

'Watch your step!' the sleek boy said. 'You'll be stepping over the edge.'

'None of your business if I did!' Meg snapped back, angry, yet drawn towards them as though against her will.

'It might upset the fish!' the rough boy said in a man's voice, loud, husky, and both boys laughed.

'You're not catching anything, anyway.'

'Oh, yes we are!'

'What are you catching?'

'Cold,' said one.

'Measles,' said the other, and they went into such exaggerated fits of laughter that we laughed too.

But I had often fought with my brother at home and had found no reason to change my opinion that boys were bullies and were to be avoided. The contempt was mutual; my brother thought girls were 'too sissy' to be worthy of notice. For the last few weeks of term I had been sitting beside a boy in school as punishment for talking in class. And so I tugged at Linda to come away; but she wouldn't budge. She stared at the boys as though she had never seen a boy before. Thinking to draw her away by going away myself, I went down to the beach and began to look for rock oysters, which, Mrs Foster had said, were sometimes to be found on the rocks at low tide.

From time to time, if I found a crab or a coloured stone, I would call to Linda to come down and see, and she would call from the wharf, 'Yes, in a minute', but she didn't come. One of the boys caught a fish and chased the girls with it, and shrieks of excited laughter floated down to where I poked among the rocks below. I had never known Linda to act so strangely. At last I grew careless with my feet, slipped on a rock and fell into the water. I was wet but in no danger, for the water was shallow; but my sunhat floated upside down out of reach, and at the sight I burst into tears. The four figures on the wharf came running to the rescue. Linda, full of self-reproach, tried to dry me with her handkerchief and the hem of her dress. The bigger boy rolled up his trousers and waded out for the hat. When they saw that I was safe, and the hat retrieved, they began to shout with laughter, all except Linda, who said, in her protective, solemn, authoritative way, 'It's not funny. She might have been drowned. A woman who was in our crib before us was drowned.' And she bustled me off home without a backward glance as though the boys were to blame.

Next afternoon, when Meg came for us, she said to me at the gate, as we left the crib, 'Peggy, you go down the cliff path, and Linda and I will go down the road, and we'll have a race to see who gets down to the bay first.'

And so I tumbled down the cliff and reached the bay before they were even in sight on the road. The bay was deserted, the boys were not on the wharf, only the water slapped on the rocks and under the boatsheds. I waited a long time; I kicked a stone about, sat in the sun on a warm rock, scanned the road for a glimpse of the girls. After a while it occurred to me that there had been time for them to go up and down the road a dozen times. I set off to look for them, and soon found myself back at the crib without having met them. Down the cliff path I ran again, and at last, after wandering haphazardly about the few roads that wound among the houses, I found them, or, rather, looked down upon them from the road above the reserve, where they walked beneath the gum trees, arm-in-arm with the two boys of yesterday. Their backs were towards me; they strolled slowly.

It was clear that whatever they were doing, they were not looking for me. I stared at Linda's brown head and blue cotton frock, unable to understand what I saw; I even wondered wildly if it could be someone else disguised as Linda. I could hear their voices, the gruff man-tones of the rough boy, who was with Linda, the shrill cries of Meg, like a gull's cries. Meg still wore her red skirt and white blouse and leaned against the sleek, dark boy. In a few moments they had passed out of view. The reserve was deserted. Some seagulls rested on the grass; a piece of white paper was lifted by a gust of wind and turned over and over like a live thing; a rustling breeze passed like a shiver over the leaves of the gum trees.

Suddenly I felt a little afraid, as though I had stumbled upon some mystery, like the mystery of the woman who had been drowned in the harbour. What had happened? I had only to call out and Linda would hear; but even at ten one hesitates to call somebody who does not want to come.

I went back to the crib to wait, where I rolled in the grass, plucking clover and composing angry speeches that I intended to deliver to Linda on her return.

A mass of sweet-peas grew outside the bedroom window on the wire-netting fence dividing our house from the next. They had been blooming uncut for a long time, and their clear colours drew me, pink, white, red, lavender, and orange-scarlet burnt by the sun. Their warm, summer scent made me feel drunk as a bee. I had a flower in my hands, examining it, when Mrs Foster tapped on the window behind me and said, 'Mustn't touch the flowers, Peggy. They're not ours.'

She opened the casement window, leaned an arm on the sill and smiled as though to show that she was not really angry with me.

'Where's Linda?' she asked.

'With Meg in the reserve with two boys,' I said.

Mrs Foster had been holding the arm of the window catch in her hand; it escaped from her grasp and the window swung wide with a clatter. She gave me a look of disgust, as though I had told a lie, or said something improper, and seemed about to dismiss me. Then her face stiffened, and as though by some trick of light, or a reflection from the leaves, her skin turned green. She searched my eyes incredulously, with a mounting fear that communicated itself to me. I could not have been more alarmed if the figure at the window had been that of the drowned woman. I saw her breast rise and fall, her nostrils widen and her prominent eyes grow strange. Then she retired into the darkness of the room and left the window swinging wide. I was overwhelmed by a feeling of homesickness; if I could have run then into the kitchen at home, nothing could have coaxed me out again.

In a few moments Mrs Foster came striding out of the house with her arms held out from her sides like the wings of an attacking bird. She carried the straw broom. She disappeared swiftly through the gate and down the road. To the reserve, there could be no doubt.

I crept into a hiding place in the gum trees over the road.

From there I watched Linda's sad return, weeping, her fists in her eyes, her head bowed, her mother, still with the broom, marching grimly behind. It was the first time I had seen Linda cry.

I stayed in the gum trees for a long time. The shadows of the trees lengthened, moved over the flowering lawn in front of the crib from which came no sound or sign of life. The air grew cold. The angry speeches I had made melted from my heart. When I crept home at last there was no anger in Linda either, or in Mrs Foster. Everyone was very subdued and polite.

Meg did not come again.

That was the last time Linda and I played together as children. In a day she had crossed over into the adult world. From then on, for her, all our games together were only excursions back into the child's world; she no longer lived in it. She had passed through the gateway through which we were all passing, late or soon, into different fields beyond. In less than two years, when she was sixteen, Linda had gone from our lives.

It was my cousin, Marion, quick and bright and careless as a bird, who brought me the news or, rather, threw it off in her flight like a drop of water, as her high heels click-clicked along the street. Marion was small and dark and vivid; she was wearing a little red hat like a pie, and with her bright eyes and sharp nose, her lipstick and rouged cheeks she reminded me of the gay birds in the aviary in the gardens. She had just turned sixteen, as Linda had, but she still seemed so much older than Linda, more neat, knowing, sophisticated. I was twelve now, and in my school uniform ran jumping beside her, for my brother and I were to have tea at her place, and I had come down to the bus to meet her as she came from work. She said, 'Did you know Linda was married?'

Married? Married? I stopped. The street scene, the road, the cyclists, the shop, with its ice-cream signs, the roughcast fence we were passing, seemed to strike me as though I fell against it.

'Of course she had to,' Marion went on, nodding significantly. 'She was on the way, you see.'

I stared at her to see if it could be true. To my surprise her face, always so assured, changed and trembled, and her eyes grew large and round, as though her thoughts were elsewhere.

'Supposing it was someone awful!' she said, not looking at me. 'Someone you did not want to marry!'

A warning seemed to pass between us. Without understanding half of what it was all about, I caught her alarm as a grazing deer will catch the alarm of another. I was in the herd, with Marion, with Linda, with Mrs Foster, with others;

as they acted, so would I have to act. If they said stand, or run, so would I have to stand or run.

'And how do you know?' Marion went on, following her own thoughts. 'How do you know you're going to go on liking him all your life? Till death do us part? How do you know that it's not going to be that you like him one time and then not another time? Some boys I used to be crazy about I can't stand now. There was Tom, and that one with the long hair who never even spoke to me.'

But I didn't want to hear her boring old list of boyfriends, and said so, and we began to quarrel.

Of course, we loved Linda's baby when he came, with his composed, sleeping features, and his minute fingers that were always making dainty, meaningless gestures. And we loved the new Linda, absorbed now in her baby and her household tasks; but the old Linda, who wanted to nurse the injured and the sick, the lepers of the world, who spoke to us of India and other countries, we never saw again. We saw the figure of a woman bent like a new moon over the baby, over the pram, over the cot, over the tub, as though she would never look up. In our lives, where she had been, there was a space like a death.

A Long Wait

Light from the kitchen shone into Mark's bedroom and woke him. Mum was up already. He could smell bacon frying and hear Dad's voice murmuring. There was something special about this morning, almost as good as Christmas morning. Dad and Uncle Jim, who was Dad's brother, had promised to take him with them, this last day of the duck-shooting season. This was the first time he was old enough to go.

'Mark! Are you awake?' Mum was calling. He jumped quickly out of bed and slipped in behind the kitchen table without looking for his clothes. Mum was wearing Dad's dressing gown. Her face was flushed with the warmth of the room. She was still wearing the hairnet she wore in bed. Dad was dressed in old clothes. 'Will you have a fried chop with your bacon?' Mum asked. 'You won't get any more food for a while.'

After breakfast Dad brought his shotgun from behind his bedroom door and sorted some ammunition on the table. Then he went down to the basement and brought up his gumboots and other gear, including some decoy ducks and two tattered old hats with wide floppy brims. The brown retriever, Nip, followed him and pushed his head against Mark's bare legs, then sat neatly, looking at the table with shining appealing eyes, hoping Mark would pass on his chop bone. He was a long-legged dog, not yet fully grown, often boisterous, but was learning to behave nicely when he was given the privilege of being admitted to the house. He soon forgot his good manners, however, and rushed suddenly to the closed door, barking officiously.

'That will be Jim,' Dad said, and ordered the dog to be quiet.

'You're not taking that pup with you?' Uncle Jim was broad-shouldered, with a weather-burned face, small black moustache and sparkling good-humoured eyes. He worked on the roads with a grader. He consistently teased Mark by dismissing Nip as 'a pup', when anyone could see that he was now as big as any other dog.

'He's a retriever,' Mark stroked the dog's head. 'He's going to retrieve the ducks.'

'How many ducks has he retrieved?' Jim's eyes twinkled, and when Mark grinned and couldn't answer, he continued, 'That pup couldn't retrieve a stick.'

He now turned to Dad and the two brothers began to discuss their plans for the day. Dad didn't have a moustache, and was not so big as Jim, although he was older. He was a carpetlayer and wore leather patches on the knees of his pants. Nip returned to his neat position beside Mark and was given the chop bone.

Mum supervised Mark's dressing, making sure that he was warmly clad. 'I'll give you extra clothes to take,' she said. 'Where there's water you are sure to get wet. I don't know how you do it. There seems to be some kind of fatal attraction.'

'How far is it to the lake?' Mark asked when he was in the back of Uncle Jim's car with Nip. Dad, who was in the front, turned to say, 'A couple of hours.'

So Mark nestled down beside the warm dog and looked out at the street lights and the dark unlit houses they were passing as they drove out of town.

The sky was changing from black to grey when they reached the lake and bumped along a grass track. The water was grey, too, with small, lighter-coloured waves breaking on a gravel beach. It was cold getting out of the warm car. An icy wind blew, rattling some flax and dry bulrushes that grew at the water's edge. No people were in sight and no houses, only distant sheep on sloping fields.

'Whose dinghy is it, did you say?' Dad asked.

'Jack MacIntosh's. You know – over the back fence. I've been out with him. It's the end of the season. He's finished with it. He says the ducks are too wary now. But we can hide in the flax round the point. There's a good stand there. I've brought the duck-caller.'

'Water looks a big choppy,' Dad said.

They stood looking out at the lake for a few moments, then went into the flax bushes to look for the dinghy. It was upside-down. They turned it over and replaced the bailing tins that had fallen out. They pushed it to the water's edge and again stood looking out at the lake.

'Not so bad here,' Jim said. 'Could be rough at the point. But once we get round there –'

They took down the oars that Jim had fastened to the roof of his car, and brought out from the boot the shotguns and other gear, including the decoy ducks. They blackened their faces with burnt cork, even Mark's, and put an old hat on his head, then pushed the boat into the water and they all got in, including the dog, who was quivering with excitement.

'Keep that dog still,' Dad said as Jim began to row.

Mark had never been in a boat. It seemed strange to take his feet off the ground and trust himself to this unsteady dinghy on a lake that stretched as far as the sky. It was not like the sea, where your feet could always touch the bottom, though it must be all right. Dad and Uncle Jim trusted it.

But as they neared the flax-covered land that Uncle Jim called 'the point', the boat began to buck up and down in a

hardly controllable manner and he grew alarmed.
'Bloody wind-change,' Uncle Jim shouted, as violent winds came from several directions at once. The waves struck against each other and tried to turn the boat round. Suddenly water was dumped in over the side. Dad picked up a can and began to bail out. He called to Mark to grab another one, but before Mark could catch the tin that now bobbed on a flood in the bottom, a wave dealt the boat a tremendous blow and turned it over.

They were all in the water. The boat was upside-down and Dad and Jim were clinging to its sides. But Mark was thrown clear and couldn't reach it. Dad yelled at him and without taking one arm from the boat stretched out his other as far as possible, but still couldn't reach him. The distance widened. Now Jim clung to the boat with one arm and stretched his other hand to Dad, who released his hold on the boat so that he could reach further. But he still couldn't stretch far enough. Then Mark felt as though some other hand had grabbed him. The dog had grasped his arm and was swimming beside him, keeping him afloat. At this, both men left the boat and all began to swim ashore. Dad and Jim and Nip, who was towing Mark with his strong jaws.

They swam towards the bulrushes where the lake was not so deep, and managed to struggle out, fighting another battle to get through the wild growth at the lake's edge. But their feet were on firm ground at last, and they were soon wrenching off their sodden clothes and receiving an unwelcome shower from Nip as he shook himself.

Shivering, and trying to hurry through the sharp and scratchy bushes, they made their way back to the gravel beach where they had left the car. There they dumped their clothes on the ground and rubbed themselves as dry as possible with handfuls of tussock and a single towel that was in the car. Dad helped Mark into the spare jersey and pants that Mum had provided, wrapped around him a groundsheet, closed him in the car and got in himself, wrapping his seat-cover round him for warmth.

'Where's the dog?' he asked.

'Rolling in the tussock.' Mark's teeth chattered.

Dad called out to Jim, who was wringing water out of the clothes and dumping them into the car's boot. 'Give the dog a whistle.'

Uncle Jim whistled piercingly, but the dog didn't come. Dad leaned out the car window and whistled too.

'We can't wait.' Jim got into the car. 'We'll have to go back and get some help for the boat.'

'We can't go without Nip!' Mark yelled.

But Jim pressed the starter and drove off without answering.

Going home in the car, missing the warm companionship of the dog, Mark cried silently. Nip would get lost, he felt sure. He would try to find his way home, but it was too far. And why wouldn't Jim and Dad speak to him? Did they blame him for taking the dog in the boat? They had said nothing at all since the accident. They thought it was his fault. Mum knew he would get wet. She said he had a fatal attraction for water. That was because he was always getting wet in the creek looking for freshwater crays. And once he had fallen into a ditch and Mum wouldn't let him back into the house because he stank so much. He had to undress in the yard and put his clothes in a bucket. And now he didn't even have Nip to love him.

Dad didn't go back with Jim to the lake. He set up his saw-bench in the backyard, dragged out some timber he had been saving and began to make an ear-splitting noise sawing it into lengths for the winter fires.

Mark lingered near him. 'How will they get the boat?' he asked in a lull in the commotion.

'They'll take another boat,' Dad said.

'How will they get it there?'

'On a trailer.'

He could not find the words to ask about Nip.

Later in the day, as he still lingered aimlessly in the yard, Dad said, 'Why are you hanging around? Get busy and stack some of that wood in the shed.'

So Mark occupied himself by carting wood to the shed, but could not stop thinking how much Nip would have enjoyed helping him. How many hours would it take Uncle Jim to get there and back? Two hours each way meant four hours. But how long would he be at the lake? Why wouldn't Dad talk about it? Was it his fault? Was he too heavy for the boat? Nip was heavy, too. Perhaps if the boat had only the two men in it, that would have been okay. Nip wouldn't know Uncle Jim was coming back to get the boat. It was cruel to leave him.

He asked Mum, 'Why won't Dad talk about it?'

'He can't,' Mum said. 'He's too angry. Don't bother him.'

Was that why he couldn't ask Dad about Nip? But he didn't feel angry. He felt sad. He couldn't ask because he knew he would cry. He sat on the step and suddenly felt sorry for Dad. He had lost his gun in the lake. He shot no ducks. He had to come home as soon as he got there. He went inside and asked Mum, 'Will Uncle Jim come back here?'

'Oh, yes.' Mum sighed. She sounded tired.

He went down the drive and looked along the street. But there was no sign of Uncle Jim's car and no sign of Nip. He had heard of dogs, and cats, too, who had made their own way home across long distances. And then he remembered that it was dark when they set out and Nip would not have seen where they were going. Never had a day seemed so long!

It was dark again when Mark heard the car in the drive and saw the lights flash on the kitchen window, where he sat at the table. He rushed outside and saw that it was Uncle Jim's car, all right. A door opened and Nip scrambled out and almost knocked Mark off his feet by jumping up on him in joyful greeting.

Uncle Jim went into the house with Dad. Mark followed after making one quick run round the yard with Nip. In the warm, bright kitchen Dad and Jim were actually laughing, and punching each other on the shoulder.

Mum set some beer and glasses on the table.

Mark gazed gratefully at Uncle Jim.

'Where did you find Nip?'

Jim's deep laugh seemed to fill the room. 'Did you lose a sock?' he asked.

Mum said, 'Yes, he did!'

'Well, that's where we found the dog.' Jim laughed again. 'He was looking after your smelly sock! He probably smelt it from a mile off.'

'He's a retriever.' Mark grinned.

'Yes, he is.' Uncle Jim ruffled Mark's hair affectionately. 'He retrieved you. Bring him with you next year in case you tip us out of the boat again.'

Everyone laughed, and by their laughter everyone knew that he was not to blame. That was just one of Jim's jokes.

So that was all right, then. They must have got the boat. There was next year to look forward to. But gee, that was going to be a long wait! A whole year!

The Macrocarpa Hedge

The evening was warm and still. Flocks of white birds rested on the sandy shores at the mouth of the river. The tide was low and the river ran smoothly, reflecting a few black broken piles, which were all that remained of an old landing stage. Larsen's store, built under a hill, was already in shadow, but the sun still shone on a faded blue farm truck across the road, where Larsen, in a white coat, had raised the truck's bonnet and was fitting a new battery.

A tall man leaned against the back of the truck, rolling a smoke. His blue pants and blue shirt had the same faded work-worn appearance as the truck, as though man and truck had spent long hours in the sun together. He had bushy, tow-coloured hair and looked about thirty. His glance moved with interest from his packet of tobacco to a stout, older woman, who stood watching him with the palms of her hands supporting her back. She was bare-legged, bare-armed, in a short red dress, and her thick black hair fanned out over her shoulders. The man made some remark that amused her, and her soft laugh travelled across the road in the stillness. He gave her the cigarette he had rolled and began to make another.

'Pam!' A man on the steps of the store called her. The two figures turned and looked at him. He held his old felt hat by the brim in one hand and a bunched handkerchief in the other. He dabbed his face with the handkerchief as though sweating. His old brown suit seemed too hot for a summer's day. 'You busy, Pam?' he asked mildly.

'Hubby wants you.' The tall man lit the two cigarettes.

The storekeeper straightened up from his work.

'What you want, Andy?' the woman asked petulantly.

'Can you spare a minute, Pam?'

Pam crossed the road slowly.

'Why doesn't Geordie give Larsen a hand?' Her husband passed his bunched handkerchief down his face and over his moustache.

'You called me over the road to say that, Andy?' She pushed her hair back from her face and looked at him resentfully. 'Geordie works for me on the farm, not for Larsen's store.'

'Hell, it was hot in the store,' Andy said.

'What you stay in there for?'

'Larsen's got in a pair of waders. They're just what I want.'

'You're always wanting something.'

'I could wade out to White Rock.'

'What you want to wade out there for?'

'They say the fishing – there's Greenbone –' Andy waved his hand towards the horizon where the dark-blue sea met the clear sky.

'You don't need to go out to that rock. What's wrong with fishing from the rocks at the point?'

'It's deep water out there.'

They both looked along the road in the direction of a great white rock that they knew stood out in the sea, though it was far out of sight, miles along the coast. The tarsealed road ended at Larsen's store. A gravel road led on to their farm and a few neighbouring farms, which had been wrested from the hard, stony country that sloped down to the sea and its rocky shore.

'Greenbone feeds on the kelp,' Andy said.

Pam drew so deeply on her cigarette that the smoke

seemed to travel down to the soles of her feet. Then she shut her mouth tight and blew the smoke fiercely through her nostrils.

'Listen,' she said. 'I've got to pay out for a new battery. I can't be paying out for boots you don't need.'

The noise of the engine drew their attention back to the truck. A few seagulls rose screaming and flew slowly towards the sea. Larsen was walking across the road to the store and Geordie, who worked and lived on the farm, was in the cab.

'Shut her off,' Pam called above the drumming of the motor, as the truck pulled up at the store. 'I'm going in for some groceries. D'you want anything, Geordie?'

Geordie thrust his bushy tow head and bare arm through the open cab window and pushed the sleeve of his shirt further above his elbow till it was stopped by his muscles.

'Two a tobacco and a couple tishies,' he said.

Pam went into the store and silence returned to the road.

'Larsen's got in a pair of waders,' Andy said to Geordie. 'Just the job for wading out to White Rock. I can't get Pam interested.'

'I didn't know you could get out to White Rock without a boat,' Geordie said. 'It's all kelp round there.'

'You can do it with waders. If this weather holds I could get over there tomorrow night. I might get some Greenbone. What about coming in and having a look at them?'

Geordie followed him into the store, but when he saw the waders he laughed.

'What size dogs do you think you got, Andy?' he asked. 'They're a mile too big for you.'

'With two pair of socks –'

'Look!' Geordie stamped his cigarette flat on the floor. 'They're a bloody sight too big for me.' His pale eyes measured them and he held them against his legs. 'But I wouldn't mind them all the same.' He took off his boots, folded his pants into his socks, and pulled them on. 'What do you think of this?' he asked Pam.

Pam rested her arms on a box on the counter and looked at him with half-closed eyes.

'Might be all right for doing a spot of ditching,' she said. 'Wouldn't do you any harm – with that pot.'

'That's all good beer.' Geordie patted his stomach, smiling, not believing he was getting a pot stomach, knowing he was lean and tall and a match for anyone.

'Right,' he said to the storekeeper, who was packing groceries into a carton, 'I'll take them. Andy 'n' I've got a fishing trip jacked up for tomorrow night.

Andy picked up the carton and carried it out to the truck. If he was disappointed, he didn't show it. On the contrary, he looked pleased.

Geordie drove home, smiling to himself, the waders on the back of the truck, Andy with his hat pulled down to his eyes, staring from the far window, and Pam wedged between. The dust from the gravel road rose in clouds behind them. Beyond the paddocks the sea, glimpsed occasionally, shone deep blue.

Only the big macrocarpa hedge, which hid all but the rusted iron roof of the old wooden farmhouse, seemed dark already with the approach of night. The huge old hedge, planted long ago to shelter the farm from the sea winds, had been kept neatly trimmed in Pam's father's time, but now had grown thick and wild. Pam had worked like a man beside Andy, when he first came to the farm to work for her father. Nothing had been the same after the old man died, Andy thought gloomily, looking at the overgrown hedge. He had married Pam, but the unending struggle against gorse and broom ... One man and one woman were not enough for such hard country, he knew, but now that Pam had taken on Geordie he was back in the workers' hut in the yard, where he had lived when he had first come to the farm. Again he was sharing the hut with Humpy, that half-witted useless old bugger who had pottered about the house and yard since Pam was a kid. Here he was now, hurrying down the path to meet them.

As the truck pulled into the yard, Humpy dramatically signalled it to stop, though it could not have gone further. He was small and white-headed and looked as thin as a stick in the apron he was wearing, which was one of Pam's, with a pattern of red flowers.

Geordie laughed boisterously. First out of the truck, he seized Humpy's arm and wrenched it high above his head. 'Directing the traffic, are you? I'll show you! Stop! Turn to the right – stop!' He began to manipulate the old man's arms like a puppet's.

'Cut that out!' Pam spoke sharply.

Geordie glanced at her and suddenly flushed scarlet. He left the old man and went round to the back of the truck and picked up the box of groceries.

'My chair broke –' Humpy was almost in tears.

'I'll come and look.' Pam moved towards the house and Humpy followed.

On the verandah, Humpy's old upholstered chair lay tipped forward, minus its front legs. Humpy could remember when his chair had been covered with gold moquette, as he had often said, but no trace of that splendour remained, except in his memory. Sun and rain had reduced the chair to a mud-coloured object that would have been thrown away long ago if it had not been for Humpy's attachment to it and Pam's attachment to Humpy.

'I picked the peas and I was shelling them.' Humpy pointed to an upset bowl of green peas.

'Here, you,' Pam said to Geordie. 'You've done this. These front legs have been sawn through. I've had enough of you and your practical jokes. You go too far.'

'Why pick on me?' Geordie laughed and ducked behind the groceries he was carrying.

'I don't see what's so funny,' Pam said. 'He could have been hurt. Why can't you leave him alone?'

Andy examined the chair,

'Can you mend it, Andy?' Humpy looked earnestly into his face for an answer. Geordie also leaned towards Andy, and repeated, in the old man's childish voice, 'Can you mend it. Andy?'

'Oh, get on!' Pam, with mock anger, pushed Geordie through the open front door and into the house.

'It's finished,' Andy said, turning away.

Humpy knelt on the verandah, gathered his apron into one hand and, with the other, began picking up the peas, not noticing that as fast as he gathered them into his apron they rolled out the other side.

Andy went on to the hut, took his accordion from the cupboard, sat on the wooden doorstep, with his back against the doorpost, and began to play over some old dance tune.

The summer twilight lingered. Humpy came to the hut, stepped over Andy's legs and stumbled against his bed. For a while he sat on the side of the bed without moving. In a lull in the music he said, 'Geordie sawed my chair so that it would break when I sat down.'

'We'll get you another chair in the morning,' Andy said.

'What sort of chair?'

'Oh, I dunno. One out of the house. We'll have to ask Pam.' Andy was playing over some of the tunes he had practised when he first took Pam to the dances in the Riverside Hall, years ago, when she was eighteen and he was thirty. He remembered them all, but Pam had forgotten them.

'Yesterday,' Humpy said, 'Geordie put two fried eggs in my porridge.'

'Take no notice of Geordie.'

'He took the knife I found under the verandah and said it was his. That wasn't true. I found it. I wanted it.'

'Well, whatever you want, if Geordie finds out, he'll take it from you. And you can count on that. Anyway, he's jealous of you, because of Pam. She should'a had kids. She goes on as if you were her little boy.'

He began to play again. The sky was still yellow in the south-west, silhouetting the house, where no light could be seen. The macrocarpa hedge was black now, dense as a building against the light-coloured paddocks.

Humpy lit the candle, undressed, pulled on a big nightgown that had belonged to Pam, folded his clothes neatly on a box and climbed into his creaking old iron bed. He lay on his back with his eyes closed. The accordion fell silent. Moths came through the open door and fluttered round the flame.

'Andy?' Humpy said suddenly. 'Why didn't you go fishing tonight?'

'We were down at the store getting a new battery for the truck.'

'Did you see Geordie's new boots?'

'Yeah.'

'What's he want those big boots for?'

'Wading out to White Rock.'

'When I was a boy we used to call that the Devil's Rock. Men have been drowned there. I've seen their names on the stones by the church.'

'That was years ago.'

'The kelp sucked them down. You know that! Nobody goes there – you wouldn't go there, would you, Andy?'

'Oh, put a sock in it, can't you?' Andy shoved his accordion aside and sat with his head in his hands.

'Aren't you going to go for your walk tonight?' Humpy asked.

Andy got up and went down the gravel drive to the road. There he walked up and down on the grass verge, the length of the hedge. Not a sound came from the darkening countryside. The macrocarpa, stored with the heat of the day, gave off a strong macrocarpa smell, as though its stems had been crushed. He turned in at the opening, where there had once been a front gate, and moved along the inner side of the hedge, hidden in its deep shadow. The light was on in the kitchen. Through the window he could see Geordie's tow-coloured head, bent over the table, where he was sorting out fish-hooks. Pam's bare arms moved across the cupboards behind him, as she stacked away the groceries. Geordie raised his head and she turned and leaned over him, touching something he showed her on the table. Her hair looked black against Geordie's head.

Andy pressed back into the hedge, in a hollow he had worn there.

A Step on the Path

In the late afternoon, when the sun had moved to the front of Myra Carter's little wooden house, there was shade to be found at the back. Myra liked to sit in a small open porch, resting her legs along the old settee, which was much scarred by standing out in all kinds of weather. She often felt tired in her retirement. The day had been extremely hot. It was impossible to continue working in the garden, though there was still much work to be done in the vegetable patch, where her parents worked when she was young. They had been dead so long now that she seldom thought of them, but still named them in her prayers and wished they could have known how grateful she felt that they had forgiven her, and left the house to her so that she might have a roof over her head when she was abandoned with the child. It was such a lovely old garden, with the pear tree near the back door, which brought blossoms and shade and fruit as the seasons changed. At this time of year the immature pears were hidden by the leaves, which were quite motionless today in the still air.

Hurried steps on the path roused her from her feeling of relaxation and she stood up. Bell Jackson from next door came round the corner carrying a box of apricots that she had promised to bring from Alexandra. This she set beside Myra on a small narrow table that had once served as a wash-stand. 'Moorpark,' she said. 'I think that's what you wanted?'

'Oh, yes, exactly,' Myra smiled happily. 'But you – it's so

hot! You must have been terribly hot in the car coming from Central.'

'Killing!' Bell sank to the end of the settee, removed her sunhat and used it to fan her face. She wore only a white sunfrock, but her bare arms and legs were red with heat. She was thirty-five and looked young enough to be Myra's daughter. Beside her, Myra, who had always been slight and in recent years had grown very thin, looked quite frail. But she was still energetic, and with her work at the woollen mills ended, turned her energies to her house and garden. She, too, wore a light loose frock, a blue floral, and looked cool in the shade. Her grey hair was straight and cut short. She took no particular interest in her appearance, but always looked neat.

'You will have something cool to drink,' she urged Bell, 'or a cup of tea?' She was very fond of Bell, thinking of her as a daughter, more so than her own daughter Ede, who had been aggressive all her life and given her a hard time. She was just as uncooperative with Gran and Pop, when they had kindly looked after her so that Myra could go back to work at the mill. Ede, when she grew old enough to take a job there, would not stay in Mosgiel, but moved to Dunedin where, she said, there was 'more life'. Now she worked for a clothing manufacturer as a cutter – a job, Myra thought, she might have found in Mosgiel in the first place.

Bell said, 'Are you going to make jam for the church fair again?'

Myra touched the box of apricots. 'This will make more than they can sell. But the Vicar knows what to do with it.'

They both smiled. But Bell would not wait for refreshment. She still had to unpack the car and make a meal for Ken, she said, and soon left.

Myra fetched the poker from the kitchen and prised up the lid of the box. The apricots were beautiful, neatly packed and clean skinned, just on the verge of ripening. She decided to make the first boiling this evening, while the sun had gone from the back of the house. Tomorrow, when the sun came in, the kitchen would be unbearably hot. She brought a stool and some bowls to the little narrow table, and split the fruit quickly and removed the stones. She still used the brass jam pan that her mother had used and which she remembered from childhood, and this she fetched from its hook in the wash-house and scoured with salt and vinegar. Then she assembled the bottles and washed them in hot water.

In the cool of the evening she built up the fire in the kitchen stove and set the weighed fruit and sugar to boil.

Only then did she sit at the kitchen table to eat her frugal meal of lettuce, tomatoes and a boiled egg, all produced from her own garden. From time to time she rose to add more coal to the fire or to stir the jam lest it should stick to the pot and burn.

She was thus peacefully occupied when she heard rapid high-heeled footsteps hurrying round the house and across the porch, and her daughter, Ede, rushed through the open back door and sank into a chair. She had a new short hairstyle and dark wisps clung to her sweating forehead, though she looked cool enough in white shorts and a top. Suddenly she burst into violent sobs.

Without asking her why she was upset, or what had brought her to drive out from Dunedin to Mosgiel at ten o'clock at night, Myra continued to stir the jam and waited for the explanation that she knew would come.

'It's Dad!' Ede cried loudly like a child.

Myra felt herself stiffen. She had not seen Chris for many years, perhaps thirty, and could hardly remember what he looked like.

'They found him –' Ede wailed. 'They found him dead in the reserve – in a dry ditch!'

'Can you remember your father?' Myra asked with some

surprise. 'Why are you so upset?'

'He was in Wellington,' Ede sobbed. 'When I was there I tried to see him. I had his address. I wanted to – I don't know what I wanted to – the woman who came to the door – a terrible trollop with a purple face and bulging eyes – said he no longer lived there. Some other man – a big guy like a bouncer came to the door behind her as though expecting trouble. I told them I wanted to find out where my father had gone – that I was his daughter – and the woman said – she said – "I don't give a tin of fish!" Imagine it!' Edie became incoherent.

Myra, seeing that Ede's handkerchiefs were saturated with her tears, passed a box of paper ones from the dresser drawer and returned to the stove. The jam was bubbling faithfully, so she poured a spoonful in a saucer and placed it in the fridge to cool.

'It was Jock Henderson told me,' Ede said. 'He knew Dad. He knew I was his daughter. Now I will never know him. Tell me what happened that you were separated?'

'We were not "separated",' Myra said. 'I went with him to Christchurch. I was abandoned with the child.'

'But why did he leave you?'

'He met another woman and just left. I tried to get work. I was treated with contempt because of the child. That's the way it was then.'

'But you were married.'

Myra fell silent.

'You were married!' Ede persisted. 'You wore a ring!'

Myra tested the jam in the saucer, poking it back and forth with a teaspoon.

'I don't think it's going to set,' she said, frowning.

Ede resumed her noisy crying. 'How can you stand there saying the jam is not going to set when your own husband was found dead in the reserve?'

'He was not my husband,' Myra said.

'Not – not –' Ede's eyes were swollen. 'I am – I am –' She rose and moved towards the door. 'I suppose he was my father?' She gave her mother a bitter look.

'Are you not going to stay the night?' Myra asked. 'Please stay the night. It's dark. It's eleven o'clock. It's too late to drive back to Dunedin. Let me make you a cup of tea.'

But Ede, scarlet-faced, not returning her mother's anxious gaze, left the way she had come, through the open door.

Myra heard her car drive away.

It was midnight by the time the jam was safely ladled into its warm jars and placed to cool on the bench. She carried the pan into the wash-house and left it to soak in the tub, then went to her room feeling the satisfaction of a task completed.

'Born in a ditch and died in a ditch,' she murmured. 'To think there was a time when I was so much in love that I trembled if he came into the dance-hall!'

She knelt by her bed. Her prayer completed, she continued to kneel and let her head fall wearily on her folded arms. 'May Ede,' she prayed, 'never shed the tears that I have shed.'

The Black Horse

Down by the bridge, on the outskirts of the town where Colley lived, the land had long been cleared and used for grazing, but only a few houses had been built there, perhaps because the river flooded. Colley's house seemed built to withstand the floods, perched as it was on high wooden piles like crutches, with a large green paddock on either side, no flowers or trees near it, only a neat lawn in front. Its whole appearance was of bareness, a bare wooden four-roomed cottage standing in bare fields, looking much the same as it must have looked when it was first built, years before.

Colley, hurrying home from school on the first hot day of summer, found his mother seated on the half-dozen wooden steps leading up to the back door, her apron full of young gooseberries which she was picking over and dropping into a bowl at her feet. She had kicked her sandals down the steps and leaned back against the post of the open door, bare-footed, bare-armed, looking hot even in the blue cotton dress she wore. She was fat and heavy and seemed slumped like a sack of wheat in the open door.

'Leave them!' She waved him off with her hand as he looked into the bowl of gooseberries. 'They'd give you a bellyache.'

She moved a little to allow Colley to step over her into the kitchen. The blinds had been pulled down and a few flies circled round the centre of the room.

'Can I go up to Scrivvy's bush for a swim?'

'Where's Red?' Her face was flushed from sitting in the sun on the back doorstep and a trickle of sweat ran down one side like a tear.

'Oh, Red's all right.'

'Wasn't he at school?'

'He's got these boils, that's all.'

'Colley!' Her voice followed him into the bedroom. 'You are not to go in the river on your own!'

He dumped his schoolbag, tugged off his shoes and socks, and muttered, too low for her to hear, 'Dry up!'

'Colley? Do you hear me?'

'Yeah.'

He changed into a comfortable old pair of shorts and a shirt that had once been blue, but had faded from many washings to a dull grey. Its soft collar had a fringe of frayed threads, which he teased out on his shoulder. He liked old clothes that were frayed and patched and had smudges of tar on them. He looked at himself in the mirror, pushed his hair up on end, put his hands in both pockets of his shorts and thrust his head forward in an aggressive manner. Could he go in bare feet? No. There were too many sharp sticks and roots waiting to snag you in the bush. He rummaged in the bottom of his wardrobe and brought out his old brown sandals, scuffed and worn, and shoved his feet into them.

The kitchen was so dark, with the blinds pulled down and his mother's large body blocking the light from the open door, that he could just make out the biscuit tin on the bench. He stuffed a few into his pockets, out of sight, and with one biscuit carried openly in his hand, stepped over his mother again and out into the sun.

'I wish I never had to go to school again, ever.'

He was walking slowly along the path, edging away, holding his hands over his bulging pockets. His mother had x-ray eyes and on some days could see right through a wall. 'Why can't you walk straight?' she said now. 'You'll grow up to be a sloucher.'

'I want to be a sloucher.'

'Where are you going?'

'Over to Red's place.'

'Then you're going up to the bush?'

'Yeah.'

'You're going for a swim?'

'It's hot enough, isn't it?'

'If Red can't go, you'll have to wait for another day.'

'OK.'

'Colley! Aren't you going to take a towel?'

'What for?'

He was round the corner of the house now, out of sight.

Over at Red's farm, on the other side of the bridge, he found Red and his mother looking along the bottom of the big hedge that ran along their drive from the road. Red had a white bandage round his neck like a dog's collar and a dark blue shirt buttoned up tight. His face looked pale under its freckles, and his light blue eyes, too, looked pale above his dark shirt. Fragments from the hedge were stuck in his ginger hair.

'What you looking for?'

'There's a hen laying somewhere along here,' Red's mother explained. She always answered for Red. She was a tall, stiff woman, with humped shoulders, and stooped awkwardly to peer among the low branches.

Colley began to look under the hedge, too. 'Coming for a dip?' he whispered to Red.

'Where?' Red straightened up as though he had been pricked.

'Where d'you think? Up at Scrivvy's bush.'

'Now?'

69

'I wasn't meaning next winter.'

Red's blue eyes shot a timid glance towards his mother. He stood very straight as though bracing himself and, in a shrill voice like a girl's, cried, 'Colley wants to know if I can go for a swim.'

'You tell Colley,' his mother said, walking slowly along the hedge, parting the branches and speaking as though Colley wasn't there, 'if you can't go to school, you can't go swimming.'

Red blushed. He turned his head aside and began to look in the hedge again.

Colley drew close to him. He pulled the biscuits out of his pockets and shared them with Red. They munched without speaking, pretending to look in the hedge, tired of looking now.

'Would you be allowed to come and watch?' Colley whispered.

'It's too far,' Red said sulkily.

'Too far? Scrivvy's bush? We've always gone there. It's the first hot day. What's the matter with you?'

'I'm supposed to stay home.' Red closed his lips primly.

'Because you've got boils? Are you going to have them all summer?'

Red lifted his head swiftly. 'Listen!'

The sound of a horse's hoofs came from the road, trotting, without haste. Colley looked up to see a black horse pass the end of the drive, ridden by a boy in a smart black riding hat. The horse trotted beautifully, his hoofs quiet on the grass verge of the road, his ears up, his long combed-out tail, which seemed almost the length of his legs, floating behind him as light as air. The rider sat straight-backed, his head held high, the peak of his cap shading his eyes, looking neither to right nor left.

Colley and Red ran out to the road. They could not see the boy's face, only his back, a tall back in a silky-looking tan shirt tucked into brown pants. He seemed older than they were.

'Who's that?' Colley breathed.

'Derek Scrivener.'

'From Scrivvy's bush? I've never seen him before.'

'He's old Scrivvy's grandson. Goes to boarding school. A proper toff. Dad says he's come to stay at his grandfather's to jump in the show.'

'On that horse?'

'Yes. The horse is called Peppy.'

'I'd give anything for a ride on a horse like that!' Colley felt his heart beat fast. 'Do you think he'd give us a ride?'

'Give us a ride? Derek Scrivener? You must be cracked! He wouldn't even let on we existed.'

Horse and rider turned with the turn of the road, trotting lightly in the direction of the bush. When they could no longer be seen, the empty country road, with its rough border of cocksfoot on either side, suddenly seemed to Colley to be unutterably dreary. Nothing, nothing, would ever come along the road again. There was nothing to see, only the stiff stems of the cocksfoot moving in the wind, and nothing to hear but the stupid crickets. It was hot. He would never have a horse like that. Red wouldn't come for a swim. Everything felt hot and wrong. He began to walk down the road towards the bush.

'Where you going?' Red asked.

He wouldn't answer.

'You're not going for a swim on your own?' Red challenged in a shrill voice.

Colley turned and glowered at Red, standing in the gateway, looking so pale and sick in his white dog's collar.

'Who's gonna stop me?' He walked on, hands in his pockets, slouching, not looking back.

At the edge of the road, on the short turf between the

gravel and the cocksfoot, he discovered many fresh prints made by the horse's hoofs. He kicked the pieces of cut turf as he walked along. The horse was new to the neighbourhood, certainly, or he would have seen it before, but evidently it was in the habit of coming this way and he might see it again.

By the time he had reached the old farm gate that led to the track through Scrivvy's bush, he was melting with heat from walking along the gravel road, and obsessed by the thought of the swimming pool in the clearing in the bush, and the ice-cold water that ran there.

The old five-barred gate was almost hidden by the high grass on this side. It had not been used for years, and its noticeboard, warning trespassers that they would be prosecuted, was overgrown by lichen. But on the other side, where the grass was grazed by cattle, the turf was short, and Colley climbed the bars and dropped into a paddock as green as a lawn. No cattle were in sight, only the twisted trees that had died in the big fire, yet refused to lie down, and by their gestures seemed still alive, huddling together in groups like people, still talking about the fire or standing out on their own, with their stumps of arms held up, signalling for help. Colley picked up a stick and whacked a few of them as he passed. The fire had gone through the bush before he was born.

This was the first time he had come here on his own. It was very quiet walking through the burnt bush without Red. Some of the old blackened trunks creaked like the boards in Red's old barn. He walked quickly, sometimes running along the top of a fallen log, or jumping from reedy hummock to hummock through the swampy places. A thumping sound accompanied him, which he discovered was the beating of his own heart.

He came out in the clearing where the grass was short

and dry with patches of clay showing through, sheltered on all sides by burnt trees lying in wreckage, or by the new, green bush with its groves of fern trees. The heat of the day seemed trapped there, coming forward to meet him like a pup, to breathe hot breath on his face and legs. The breath smelled of sun-baked grass and the bush itself, with its odour of moss and black earth. A few manuka shrubs marked the course of the river, which lay hidden under its clay banks, but the clearing, close-cropped by cattle and rabbits, was as open and sunny as a football field.

He raced over the grass and saw with joy that the pool, glistening in the sun, was unchanged from last summer. It was the only pool in the river deep enough and clear enough for swimming. Further downstream the river was spoilt by weeds which, in some places, reached out from either bank till they met in the middle, but here, where the water ran fresh out of the bush, amber-coloured, sparkling like ginger ale, you could see every stone on the bottom. The quick currents had scooped a clean hollow in the gravel, taking a half-circular sweep before moving on. He flung his stick in and watched it bump against the bank before sailing out of sight.

He threw off his shirt and shorts and waded in. The water was sharp-cold and made him catch his breath. There was only one way to get under and that was to drop yourself in. He held his nose and sank till he felt the cold close over his head, then sprang up again like a cork. He gasped. Delicious water! He struck out in a few swimming strokes. If Red had been here, he would have splashed him. He would surprise Red by coming here every day as long as Red was sick, and then, when Red came, he would show him how far he could swim. Soon the water no longer felt cold; it lifted him and carried him. He kicked out, showing the water what he could do. But the water was alive, too, and pushed against him with

its currents till he was panting for breath. He had to fight his
way back upstream. But by starting at the top of the pool he
found he could float blissfully, without effort, from one end
to the other. Lying on his back, he sailed along under a blue
sky that had only a few smudges of windy cloud in it like
smudges of chalk made by sweeps of a duster over a
blackboard.

A sound that he thought at first was distant thunder grew
into the galloping of a horse's hoofs and made him feel with
his feet for the bottom of the pool. The water was too deep,
and he almost went under, but a few strokes brought him
nearer the bank, where he found he could touch the gravel
with his toes and keep his head and shoulders clear.

The black horse that he had seen earlier, from Red's gate,
was being pulled up sharply on the bank, his hoofs striking
the ground heavily, half-shying, almost out of control. The
boy in the tan shirt was carried round in a circle as he
tightened rein. His face was as red as a plum, his eyes rolling
like the horse's eyes. He was shouting in the direction of the
pool: 'Hey, you there! What the bloody hell do you think
you're doing?'

Colley stared at the shining black horse with the floating
tail that nearly reached the ground, his pointed, turned-back
ears. His sides heaved, as though he had been ridden hard;
he was excited and difficult to quieten. The boy gripping the
reins had large hands and looked well able to control him,
but was carried round in a circle again. He was a bigger boy
than Colley, perhaps fifteen, and dressed up in tonky clothes
– that silky tan shirt and smart black riding hat.

'Do you hear me?' he yelled at Colley as the horse stood
still. Colley was silent.

The boy said again, menacingly, 'What do you think you're
doing?'

'Baking a cake,' said Colley, looking at him boldly.

'Don't you know you're on private property?'

'Prai-vite property?' Colley mimicked the boy's boarding school accent. 'Oh, ai say!'

'This is my grandfather's property. Don't you know where you are?'

'Old Scrivvy's bush.'

'Why, you – you –'

The boy dismounted and made a dramatic gesture with one arm, pointing like the burnt trees behind him. 'Come out or I'll fetch you out!'

'Lord Scrivener's bush,' Colley said, laughing.

Suddenly it seemed to him that the boy ought to laugh, too. The river was laughing, the sun was shining, it was a laughing kind of day. 'Come and have a swim,' he invited, grinning widely. 'The water's beaut.'

The boy's eyes bulged and rolled as though he, too, like the horse a moment before, would shy and kick the ground. He pulled off his shirt and pants and the sporty-looking hat, and keeping on his very white, new-looking underpants, began to wade into the river. His legs were surprisingly hairy, his arms long and ape-like as he swung them from side to side at the bite of the cold water.

Colley began to splash him defiantly, beating up fountains.

The boy came on, not splashing Colley in return, but keeping his crazy-looking bulging dark eyes fixed on him.

He was almost upon him. It was time to quit. Colley struck out for the bank behind him. As he kicked out he felt his leg caught in a tight grip. Angry, he turned and kicked the boy in the stomach with his free leg and the boy let go. He felt for the gravel bottom with his toes. In that instant the boy threw his arm round his neck and ducked him.

Colley was face down in the water, holding his breath, struggling, the weight of the boy pressing him down. He lashed out in a fury, trying to get his opponent off balance, but the boy held him under. Suddenly Colley knew he was in real danger. The boy meant to drown him. He felt his lungs burst and the water choke him.

From a distance he could hear someone coughing, coughing, coughing. Slowly he realised that it was himself he could hear. The noise, the distress, was issuing from his own body. He did not know how he had reached the bank, but he lay on grass, with green blades close to his eyes and someone was thumping him on the back, knocking the water out of him. He tried to rise, and vomited.

Turning on his side, he saw the big boy's face come into focus, bent over him, tears spilling from his dark eyes and running down his cheeks.

Colley sat up.

There was something wrong with the boy. He was blubbering like a girl.

'I – I didn't mean –' the boy stammered, shrinking back as Colley looked at him.

Colley coughed up more water. The ground, the trees, reeled sickeningly.

The boy brushed the tears from his face with his hand and walked slowly towards his own small heap of clothes that lay on the grass. He picked up his brown pants and felt in their pockets.

'Here,' he said, coming back to Colley and kneeling on the ground. 'Look here.' On the grass he set out a flat metal pocket knife, a compass and a red torch as small as a pencil, which he switched on and off to show that it worked. 'I'll give you anything you want.'

Behind the glint of metal something moved over the grass, a horse's mouth and hoofs and a shadow. The black horse was grazing near as he waited and wandered.

'Would you like a ride?'

'You wanted to drown me,' Colley said huskily. His throat felt sore.

The boy covered his face with his hands.

'Honest – I don't know –'

Behind the boy's hunched shoulders Colley could see the burnt trees and the green places where the ferns grew. Nobody ever came to the clearing. He was alone with the big boy. Something had happened; the place felt harsh, like a place of punishment. He had wanted a ride on the horse, but not now.

The boy took his hands from his face and said without looking up, 'Promise – you won't tell?'

But Colley was thinking, 'What if he chases me – a big boy like that with long legs?' He looked around for his clothes, got up, rolled his shorts and shirt into a bundle, and without waiting to put on his sandals slipped quickly across the clearing towards the cover of the bush.

Glancing back, he saw that the boy was still kneeling on the ground.

The Other Room

Today, when I was walking along a street in Lower Hutt, I passed a house that I first visited with my father, when I was fourteen. The house, which was wooden with a corrugated iron roof, had not changed, except that it had grown older, and some large shrubs now grew close to it, in its small front garden. I knew that it was now occupied by strangers, but I passed it slowly. I wondered, would I find the trellis summer-house still standing, sagging even more under the weight of its giant honeysuckle vine? Did the crooked apple tree still grow in the back garden? The summer-house built against the end of the house was three-sided, open to the sun. Rod used to sit there till he was sunburned, the wheels of his chair resting on a square weather-bleached carpet which lay spread on the concrete.

The summer-house overlooked the path to the back door, and it was there, as I came round the house with my father, that I first saw Rod, seated in his wheelchair, with a green rug over his knees. He was middle-aged, with a heavy face and neck, and looked extremely strong. He seized my father's hand between both of his, and said 'Pete!' and seemed unable to say more. Then, quite suddenly, he threw back his head, filled his lungs, and gave a tremendous shout. 'Annie!'

A woman appeared at the open back door, bright-eyed, alert. She gave an exclamation of recognition and came out to the summer-house, walking lightly. She was thin and tall. Her shoulders and hip bones showed through her brown jersey and skirt. Her hair was dark, skimpy, and gathered to the back of her head. She seated us on some green kitchen chairs that stood in the summer-house, and sat at a little distance apart, in the deepest shadows of the honeysuckle vine. She followed with interest the conversation that sprang up between Rod and my father, which was mainly about people and events in her old home town, but she seemed to merge with the brown vine, and listened in silence.

The two men were talking of days before I was born, of people I did not know. My attention wandered to the crooked apple tree that grew in the centre of the back lawn. I thought its shape was interesting and I should have liked to draw it. The trunk was as bare of branches as a palm tree but, unlike a palm, it had tried at least three different directions while growing. The branches at the top were scanty and spread like the framework of an umbrella. White blossoms shone on its sunny side and, from time to time, petals floated down.

Annie's sister, Isobel, came home from work and joined us. She worked in an insurance office and was so unlike Annie that I found it hard to believe the two women were sisters. She wore a fashionable pink dress and pearls, and was solid and square, and more grey than Annie, though she was younger. I discovered from the conversation that there was a still younger sister, Denise, who was married and living in Auckland. Isobel was not married. She brought out a photograph of Denise's two children.

'Walker and Virginia,' she said, showing us the head and shoulders of a young man with an open face, and his plump, smiling sister. 'When I build my house I shall have room for them to come and stay. And that's not so far off. I've been saving a long time now.' Her mouth looked twisted when she spoke.

'Seth still comes,' Annie said.

'Oh, yes,' Isobel laughed. 'Seth's still around. You

wouldn't believe it. I don't know why he doesn't take off.'
She blushed, colouring in her throat as well as in her face.
'I don't know what we would do without Seth,' Annie said.
It was Isobel who saw us off at the gate, muttering to my
father, out of the side of her twisted mouth, 'I couldn't begin
to tell you. The bugger won't let her out of his sight. The
abuse – the language –' She covered her face with one hand.

I looked back, before we turned the corner, on our way
to catch the train at the station, and saw her still standing at
the gate. Her pink dress showed up brightly against the
background of dull wooden houses, which all seemed to be
alike, with closely curtained windows, corrugated iron roofs,
and small patches of front garden. Among some of the houses
a few large tree ferns grew.

'Twenty years,' my father said, 'Rod has had that creeping
paralysis. He left Greymouth in search of treatment, but
nothing can be done for him.'

I was surprised, when I called on Annie and Rod again,
ten years later, when I was once more passing through
Wellington, to find that everything was much the same as on
my first visit, except that Rod was now in bed and not able to
get up. In that interval I had grown up, married and had two
children, and my father, who had walked away from Rod's
house so freely that sunny spring day, had been dead for eight
years.

The large summer-house, where Rod sat so long, still
supported the great honeysuckle vine and was stored with
garden tools, a lawnmower, and Rod's empty wheelchair. The
crooked apple tree still held up its umbrella spokes on the
back lawn and had just recently dropped its leaves. Annie's
hair showed strands of grey. Her shoulders were stooped,
but she still walked lightly and easily. I was led at once into
the bedroom.

Rod, pale-skinned, older, remarkably heavily built in the shoulders, was propped high on pillows. A newspaper was spread open in front of him on a special stand, like a large music stand.

'What do you think of this, eh?' he asked me. 'Seth has rigged it up. I must have my papers. I like to know what's going on in the world.'

'He knows more about the world than I do,' Annie said.

'You came with your Dad, last time,' Rod said.

'Yes. I didn't bring the children. They are too restless.'

'So Pete's gone,' Rod said, not looking at me, but turning over in his mind some memory of his old friend. 'Can you tell me what became of old Doug McIntosh? I used to go out fishing with him.'

'That must have been before my time,' I said.

'Doug McIntosh and his wife, Biddy – they lived in that old house on the corner – it had a brick fence with ivy –'

'I remember that house with the brick fence and ivy. It's down now. There's a shop on that corner.'

'So the old house is down. Doug McIntosh must be gone.'

From the bedroom ceiling hung ropes and rings Rod had once been able to use to hoist himself up in bed, but these were tied out of the way. Had Seth rigged them up, I wondered? How did Annie manage to lift him up in bed? Did Isobel help her? When did Seth come? Did he still come?

Rod had moved from Greymouth before I was born. There was little I could tell him to interest him. It was thirty years since he had lived there. He wanted information that I was not able to give him. When he realised this, I saw a frustrated and ferocious gleam in his eyes. The conversation was easier when he turned to news of the day. Annie went to the kitchen to make tea, and before long moved me to the living room, where she had spread a lace cloth on one end of the table and set out afternoon tea.

Isobel spread out on the other end of the table a builder's plans for her new house. She had retired from work.

'Plenty of cupboards,' she said. 'And, you know, Walker and Virginia, my nephew and niece, have never been down here. They are both married. Denise and the father are on their own. If I had a place for them to come and stay – Well, now, this is where I am going to have the electric range, in line with the bench.'

'Annie!' Rod shouted from the other room.

Isobel shrank from the direction of his voice. Annie slipped away, carrying tea and scones for him.

'You know Annie had to give up going to work?' Isobel said. 'She went for an hour or two in the evening, to a corner shop. It took her out of the house. She saw other people. I was here. Seth was here. The bugger stopped it. He won't let her out of reach. A while ago she was not well. I wanted him to go into a nursing home so that she could take a holiday – only for a fortnight. She has not been away from the house for thirty years.'

She fell silent, leaning on her hands, forgetful of the house plans that lay in front of her.

'It didn't get as far as asking him,' she went on after a while. 'Annie wouldn't hear of it. She said it was no use. It would make a row. She thinks he will die. But he's so strong! You hear his voice? He will outlive her!' She looked at me with shocked eyes. 'No! No!' she continued. 'It mustn't end like that. I want this new house for Annie when Rod goes. This is her room – here –' She tapped the plans with her forefinger. 'And this is my room and this is the spare room for Denise or for the young people. Three bedrooms and a lounge –' She broke off, rolled up the plans and pushed them aside. 'But Annie will die first,' she said. 'He has worn her to the bone.'

She poked up the fire, added coal from a copper scuttle,

drew her chair close to it, and spread her hands in an attempt to warm them at the smoking coal.

'I hate him!' she said, flashing a bitter glance in the direction of his room. 'I couldn't bear to have him touch anything of mine. I could be the first to die. If I leave the house to Annie –'

I sought for something to say to Isobel, but could think of nothing. I sat by the table, where Annie had arranged the afternoon tea on the lace cloth. Looking round the room, I became aware of details I had not noticed before. Isobel's chair, where she crouched over the fire, was upholstered in tan velvet, without arms, low in the seat, and high-backed. Annie's chair, opposite, was a wooden kitchen chair, painted green, not an easy chair, but one from which she could rise quickly. On the wall, above a dark cupboard, hung a framed brown photograph of Rod as a young man, standing beside a bicycle. In a row, along the back of the cupboard, stood photographs of Denise's children, Walker and Virginia, taken at various ages, including one of Virginia in her wedding gown. The table stood beside a window that overlooked the back lawn and the skeleton apple tree, with its brown leaves lying underneath it like a dropped garment.

Annie came back into the room in her noiseless fashion.

'Do you get any apples from that tree?' I asked.

'A few,' she said. 'It's a Cox's Orange.'

'It has the blight,' said Isobel, from the fireplace.

A figure passed the window. A large man was coming to the back door with a cauliflower in his hands. Giving a light knock, and calling out 'Hello?' he passed through the kitchen and entered the room and sat down on a dining chair just inside the door, with the practised movements of someone who was in the habit of coming in. He no longer carried the cauliflower, evidently having put it down somewhere on the way. Isobel did not look up from the fire.

'You've met Seth?' Annie asked me and, when she found that I had not, she introduced me as 'Pete's youngest, from the coast'. She brought another cup of tea from the kitchen and drew the sugar bowl towards him on the table.

Seth was a very large man.

'I'm sorry I missed seeing Pete that last time he came,' he said. 'How long ago was that?'

'Ten years,' I said.

'If I had known it was the last time –'

'Who could know that?' Annie said. 'Pete looked so well.'

Seth sugared his tea and ate a scone in silence.

'We came one afternoon,' I said. 'That was the last time we were in Wellington. I think you were at work.'

'Seth's got his own carrying business now,' Annie said. 'He comes in every evening.'

'I had a job out this way today,' Seth said. 'I've got a tip for Rod.'

'Then you'd better go and tell him,' Isobel said, sourly.

'It's for the last race on Saturday,' Seth said, not looking at Isobel. He was wearing clothes that were too large even for him. The sleeves of his jersey hung over his wrists and his enormous trousers hung over his shoes. He pushed his empty cup aside and sat with a hand on each knee, looking at nothing, as a man might sit in a doctor's waiting room, waiting to be called. He held his head tilted to one side, listening.

They were all listening, I now realised: Seth, Isobel and Annie, listening for Rod's shout from the other room, the room that was out of sight, but never out of mind.

Three years later I was again in Annie's living room, and for all the change in the furniture, the photographs, the view of the crooked tree on the lawn, which was bare and wet because it was winter, my absence might have been no more than three days. But now Isobel's tan velvet chair was empty and stood against the wall. Isobel was dead and so was Rod. Isobel had died three months before Rod. Annie lived alone.

I had brought some recent photographs of old friends of Annie's. She put on a pair of glasses and looked at them, asking a few, not many, questions about their children and grandchildren. Her hair was now white, but still brushed back from her face and fastened in a tiny bun. She no longer sat on a straight-backed kitchen chair, but on a comfortable old cane chair that had stood in the bedroom.

'Rod died like a fly on a pin,' she said, passing back the photographs.

I became aware of the silence in the room and of the ticking of the old brass-faced clock that stood on the mantelpiece. Memories of my last visit haunted me. Isobel had seemed so strong, standing by the table, spreading out the plans for her new house.

'Are you going to stay here?' I asked.

Annie stared absently at the fire. 'Isobel didn't get her new house built. She knew she would go before Rod. She was afraid we would both go before Rod. She had saved a lot towards her house. She left the money to Denise's children, Walker and Virginia. Not that they ever came down from Auckland, even for her funeral. I used to think Seth and Isobel – But nothing came of it. Seth is getting older, too, of course. But he still comes in.'

The New Teacher

Vonnie was the last passenger in the bus. Although she wore only cotton shorts and a loose shirt, she felt uncomfortably hot, so moved forward to sit behind the driver to catch some of the air that blew in through his open window. For a long time the bus had been climbing through steep brown sunburnt hills, but now it was descending to flat green fields where sheep and cattle grazed and a few isolated farmhouses could be seen among dark trees. A faint smell of crushed grass and sheep yards drifted through the window, reminding her of the sheep and cattle in pens at the summer show in town, where she had gone with Bronwyn on just such a hot day. Bronwyn won a box of chocolates at a booth by knocking down pegs with a ball and they sat in the shade of the grandstand eating so many chocolates they both felt sick and had to go home without having a ride on the Ferris wheel. She felt sick now, but could not tell whether it was from the heat and travel or apprehension about going to her first job.

'Is it much further?' she asked the driver.

'Pukeko at four,' the driver shouted over his shoulder. 'You the new teacher?'

'Assistant,' she said.

'They always board at Mick Anderson's. That's where you said you want to get off.' He made a sweeping movement with one arm. 'Used to be all bush down here on the flat. Good dairy country now.'

Bronwyn was always the lucky one, Vonnie reflected, so lucky to get an appointment in Christchurch, while she was on her way to a little school in the country. This was the first time they had been parted since Bronwyn had come to live in her street when she was seven and Bronwyn nine. It gave her a homesick feeling to think of their separation. She would write to her and tell her everything that happened. She would have to write to Mum, too, who had tears in her eyes when she saw her off on the bus.

'That's Anderson's place.' The driver pointed to a red-roofed farmhouse that stood alone a little distance from the road in a field without trees. A large number of black and white cattle stood close together between the house and some outbuildings. The house looked bare and lonely and Vonnie could see no building that resembled a school.

'Milking time,' the driver said, setting her bags on the side of the road beside a railed gate.

With the departure of the bus in a cloud of dust, Vonnie realised she was now here, at the house where she was to board. A grassy gravel road crossed the field where the cattle stood, leading from the gate to the house, but she could not – simply could not – follow the road through those big heavy animals. They were not all cows; that great black one with a ring in his nose, looming among them like a big black elephant – that was a bull! She looked around helplessly. Nobody had come to meet her. No one had even noticed the bus as it rumbled off. The deserted road, the scorching heat, the smell of the nearby cattle and the thud of their occasional hoof movements pressed upon her. There was no shade where she could shelter from the sun; all seemed hot, foreign and bewildering.

The cattle began to move uneasily. A small boy was making his way through them, yellow-haired, red-cheeked, smiling eagerly. 'You the new teacher?' he asked, unfastening the chain that held the gate. 'I'm Graham. Mum says come up to the house.'

'There's a bull –' she pointed.

The boy's smile widened to a grin. 'That's only William. He comes up with the cows to be milked. We put him through the bails.' Without bothering to close the gate again, he took hold of the bull by the ring in his nose and led him aside. 'We had Miss Kirkland before. She got married. We gave her a table lamp with a pink shade.' He picked up her bags with obvious pleasure and led her through.

Mrs Anderson was a stout strong-shouldered woman of about middle age. She sent the boy away to the milking shed and ushered Vonnie into a large old-fashioned kitchen, which contained a very large scrubbed wooden table covered at one end with a white cloth set for afternoon tea. On the floor knelt a young woman in a brown frock and coarse brown woollen stockings shelling broad beans on to newspapers which had been spread around her. A pair of light blue eyes looked up. A face that was child-like, yet too old for a child, broke into a broad smile. Her arms waved apparently uncontrollably.

'This is Nina,' Mrs Anderson said. 'She's shelling beans for me. She's spastic but she likes to help.'

The bedroom was cool and tidy with an open sash window and blue bedspreads on two single beds. A massive wardrobe stood in one corner and beside it a dressing table and an old-fashioned wash-stand supporting a china basin and jug.

'I have to go out to the cows,' Mrs Anderson said. 'Please make yourself at home. You might like to walk up to the school? Keep to the road and you will see the school on your right, past the Pukeko Hall.'

Vonnie crossed to the window. Nothing to see but a black dog asleep in the heat, stretched full length at the door of an old shed and, beyond that, a dark hedge and distant hills that looked blue in the afternoon light.

Mrs Anderson reappeared at the open door wearing a sacking apron, woollen cap and gumboots. 'I've poured you a cup of tea,' she said cheerfully.

In the kitchen, Nina, shuffling around on her knees on the floor, made sounds and gestures as though trying to speak, but nothing intelligible emerged. Vonnie interpreted a few repeated arm movements as a command to sit at the table.

'I am going to look at the school,' she found herself shouting at Nina after eating scones and jam. Why was she shouting, she wondered? The girl wasn't deaf, was she? Did she spend her whole life kneeling on the floor?

Nina smiled widely and waved an arm loosely but persistently in the direction of the school.

To reach the road Vonnie found that again she had to cross the paddock with the cows, but now they had moved closer to the sheds and there was space left for her. The bull was not in sight. She picked her way nervously, keeping close to a wire fence, planning to slip through the wires if he reappeared. Safely out on the road, she was struck again by the intensity of the heat and disliked the feel of the rough gravel underfoot, but was anxious to see the school where she was to work with a Mr Reid. She passed a barn-like building marked 'Pukeko Hall' and, surprisingly, a tennis court, then could see, a little further on, a building that was unmistakably the school, a small, high wooden structure painted yellow. Beside it, half-hidden by a thick hedge and also painted yellow, stood the school-house where Mr Reid lived, an old settled-looking house, with large trees behind it. Everything stood out clear and sharp, the adjoining fields and a purple tinge in the sky above the distant hills, and a design like a human face on the iron knocker as she raised it.

A tall young man with penetrating blue eyes introduced himself as Watty Reid and, taking a large key from behind the door, invited her to come and view the school. He strode quickly across a playing field where the dusty grass was bare in patches, expecting her to follow, not realising that she had to hasten to keep up with him.

'There was some talk of closing down the school,' he said as he opened the door, 'but we managed to save it – in the meantime, anyway. The roll has fallen, but the children already have to travel some distance from their farms and it would be very hard on them if they had to go any further. This is your room –'

It looked unusually bare for a schoolroom, with the walls still clad in the original dado painted brown and quite unadorned except for a few maps. She would alter this bareness, she decided at once. She would ask the children to paint pictures for the walls and pin them up so that everyone could enjoy them. Bright colours were needed – and poems copied out with bright crayons. She would encourage them to write poetry. The pictures and poems would hang side by side. She would bring the children out of themselves – teach them to express themselves in art. They would love her for it and she would love them. A feeling of happiness flooded her. She saw their heads bent over the desks, little country boys and girls.

'Have you ever lived in the country?' Mr Reid asked.

She shook her head dreamily.

'It's bloody cold here in winter,' he said. 'We're in the shade of the trees. But we have stoves, as you see. I don't want to talk shop on your first day – though I want to tell you to establish your authority from the beginning. These youngsters are very independent. They are used to bossing animals and don't like to be bossed themselves. You must make it clear who's boss. It's the animals, you see.'

What had animals to do with school? Vonnie stroked her damp hair back from her forehead and looked wonderingly at Mr Reid, who stood swinging the door key on one finger. She had no intention of bossing the children. That was not what she had been taught. She walked up to the desk that was to be hers and thought of trying the chair, but felt his eyes anxiously regarding her.

'It's all ready for you,' he said. 'Miss Kirkland cleared out the drawers.'

She opened the top drawer. Inside lay something grey like an old floor-cloth. It was a rat! She shrieked and retreated to the wall.

Mr Reid leapt to the drawer. 'It's dead! It's all right – it's dead!' He pulled the drawer out and carried it around as though not knowing whether to rush outside with it or to stay and reassure her. 'It's the boys – It's a joke –' He dashed outside.

Coming back with the empty drawer, he said, 'You see what I mean? You were supposed to discover this in class.' He turned it upside down, tapped the bottom and slipped it back into the desk. 'I don't think it would have died there by itself,' he muttered darkly.

A sudden clap of thunder broke overhead.

'There's a storm coming,' he went on. 'It was too hot to last. Come back to the house with me.'

Outside thunder clouds had darkened the sky and heavy drops of rain began to fall.

'I'll run for it,' Vonnie said. She heard his vehement protests, but ran from him, from the school, from that horrible drawer. She wanted to run and run and never stop, hardly noticing the sharp stones on the gravel road that pressed against her light shoes. Halfway back to the farm the rain descended in sheets, pelting her, drenching her to the skin. She gasped as she ran, feeling the coldness and wetness of it, but suddenly found she did not care. Let it rain. She was so wet now the rain no longer mattered. As soon as she got indoors she would have a hot shower and change her clothes.

At the farm the cows had gone from the field. She squelched through wet mud to the house and found Mrs Anderson just inside the back door wiping eggs with a cloth and placing them in a tray on the bench. She looked quite dry and peaceful.

'I'm soaked!' Vonnie paused on the step. 'May I have a hot shower?'

'We have a bath, but not a shower.' Mrs Anderson glanced at her briefly, then continued to wipe the eggs. 'I'm sorry there's no hot water – we have to light the copper in the wash-house to get hot water for a bath. You'll find some clean towels folded on top of the copper. A good rub down with a towel and some dry clothes will fix you up.' She held an egg close to her eyes and examined it shortsightedly.

So, there were to be no early morning showers before school, Vonnie thought miserably, as she peeled off her wet clothes and rubbed herself with a towel.

Mrs Anderson passed the wash-house window supporting Nina under the arms, half-carrying her, undeterred by the rain. What a weight to lug about! Yet she was actually laughing as they both disappeared into the little wooden-box lavatory at the end of the yard.

'We have dinner at midday,' Mrs Anderson said, as she set the table for tea and invited Vonnie to be seated. Mr Anderson sat at the end of the table and smiled warmly, his eyes glancing brightly from under thick black eyebrows.

'You will be able to keep your eye on our boy, Graham,' he said, 'and see that he does his homework.'

Graham, slipping into a chair beside her, blushed and bent his head. His mother sat opposite, feeding Nina, who had been placed in a high chair and had a towel wrapped round her neck. With each spoonful of some kind of soft food, the mother put her arm around Nina's head and held her still against a shoulder while she popped the spoon into the girl's mouth with the quick action of a bird feeding its young.

The father seemed thoughtful. He cut himself a slice of bread from a loaf on the table, spread it with butter and jam and added a wedge of cheese. Sighing, he said, 'I'm afraid that's the end of old Bob. He won't recover. I shall have to shoot him.'

Nina's eyes flashed suddenly and she threatened her father with wild arms.

'Don't upset Nina,' Mrs Anderson said. 'We don't want to hear about that.' She glanced at Vonnie. 'Bob is an old horse,' she explained. And then, as though anxious to change the subject, said, 'One of our married daughters is staying here with her husband. They are in town today but will be back later. I have put Nina in your room – just for a night or two. They are staying here till Friday. We are having a party for Nina on Thursday — she will be twenty-one.'

'I have a friend –' Vonnie blurted. 'Bronwyn – she turned twenty-one a week ago today. The same age –' she ended weakly and waved her knife as though Nina's movements had affected her.

'She had a party?' Mrs Anderson prompted, and receiving no reply, went on, 'We're holding Nina's in the Pukeko Hall. We're getting a band from town. Nina loves socials. People are coming from miles around.'

Vonnie murmured something, she hardly knew what. It was too horrible – to be twenty-one and still on the floor in coarse woollen stockings like an infant at the crawling stage. Bronwyn's age! A tear ran from her eyes and she brushed it away with a finger. She imagined herself crying at the table, at her first place, her first night!

'I have made a fire in the front room,' Mrs Anderson said. 'If you want to do any book work you're welcome to go up there – it's quiet. We are used to teachers.'

Vonnie placed her writing pad on the round oak table in the front room, where everything looked old-fashioned, dark and seldom used, but comfortable, especially with a bright wood fire burning in the large fireplace. She welcomed the retreat it offered, but felt terribly homesick. She would not write to Bronwyn – she would write home. '*Dear Mum,*' she began, then paused, sucking the end of her pen and thinking over the events of the day. It was all a terrible mistake, she decided, and wrote, '*I don't think I am cut out to be a teacher after all.*'

She could hear something in the passage, the sound of Nina shuffling along on her knees, and it frightened her. Nina was not a child; she was a woman – Bronwyn's age. The door opened and Mrs Anderson looked in. 'Nina wants to play something on the piano for you,' she said, and retreated.

Nina, nodding and beaming, scraped along to the piano in the corner, and still kneeling, and with concentrated attention, brought the wild movements of her arms under sufficient control to pick out, with one finger, a tune.

Vonnie recognised a song she had learnt to play as a child. Nina still had a child's soft fair curls, which reminded her of children she had seen in class trying so hard to succeed. She began to fit the words to the tune, and sang slowly, in time with Nina's playing, '*When we grow old, Let us recall these happy hours and hold …*' She remembered all the words and sang the song twice while Nina played.

Nina's delight radiated from her face. Chuckling, nodding, she shuffled out of the room as she had come, on her knees and bottom.

What had happened to the girl, Vonnie wondered. An

accident at birth? Then she thought suddenly, 'That could be me!'

She screwed up her letter and threw it into the fire. Taking another page, she wrote:

Dear Mum,

Just a line to let you know I arrived safely. It was very hot in the bus. After I got here we had a thunderstorm and rain and now the weather has turned cold. The Andersons have made me very welcome. I have been to see the school and will tell you more about that later.

Love, Vonnie.

P.S. There is a horse here that is going to be shot.

The Visitor

An old woman lowered herself carefully down the half-dozen steps at the back door of her wooden cottage, steadying herself against the hand-rail, which swayed a little under her weight. The bottom step was missing, but she climbed down with the aid of her strong walking stick. She was very stout, very old, lame, bent almost double. A strand of grey hair had fallen over her eyes, and this she pushed aside slowly, showing a square heavy face that looked as grey and weather-beaten as old stone. Crossing the square of uneven asphalt at the back door, she peered towards a patch of bright colour she could see at the bottom of the vegetable garden. She was wearing her best dress, a black silk with a pattern of red flowers, and had tied a faded cotton apron over it to keep it clean. On her feet were a pair of worn-out slippers with holes cut for her bunions.

The sight of the long, tufted, weed-grown path that led down the centre of the vegetable garden made her hesitate. She glanced from the scissors she carried in her hand to the patch of colour at the bottom of the garden and back to the scissors again. But at length she began to make a slow, ungainly snail-like progress along the overgrown path between the jostling rows of vegetables.

It was almost noon, on a hot day of summer. The sun drew a strong odour from the lanky weeds that were taking possession of the garden, and from the cabbage bed, where some of the cabbages were rotting. At the end of the path, in a bed of their own, as though they, too, were vegetables, grew some neat rows of gladioli. Each plant, with its bayonet-like leaves, had been securely staked and labelled; but now the labels were half-hidden by weeds. Five gladioli were in bloom, one scarlet, two apricot, one pink and one white. These the old woman cut with her scissors. Then she cut a few green branches from a bush by the fence. The sheaf of flowers was awkward to carry in addition to her scissors and walking stick. She stumbled a few times, but did not fall. When she had left the rough path she walked more steadily. Back at the house she filled a bucket with water and placed the flowers in it, on the floor by the sink.

Her kitchen faced the west and was dark in the mornings, and still cool, though a small fire burned in the black stove. Setting one foot inside the fender to brace herself, for the stove was very low, she removed a couple of rings from the top with a poker and placed above the embers a mutton chop secured in an old-fashioned wire toaster. Then she lifted the lid of a small pot, satisfied herself that it was still boiling, and poked with a fork the solitary potato it contained. Moving slowly, her weight causing the floorboards of the old wooden house to creak under her feet, she spread a blue cloth on the table and brought knife, fork, pepper and salt from an oak dresser that was so large it covered almost the whole of one wall. The only other furniture in the room was a wooden-backed kitchen sofa and four straight chairs painted blue.

The fire began to spit and splutter as the fat on the chop melted and dripped. The old woman pulled a chair to the fender and sat holding and turning the chop in its wire cage. From time to time she raised her head and glanced out of the window, from which she could see nothing but the sun-soaked weatherboard wall of the house next door, which was a replica of her own, and of most of the houses in the street, a four-roomed cottage with a verandah across the front.

After her meal, which she had finished by the time the old brass-faced clock on the mantelpiece struck twelve, and when she had washed her dishes, she fetched a bus timetable from the drawer of the dresser and studied it carefully, holding it up to the light from the window and very close to her eyes.

A man with his shoulders up and head forward passed the window and mounted the back steps. He filled the open doorway, a large man about sixty-five, with a big nose and small eyes that were screwed up almost out of sight. He wore a straw hat and his face was brick red and perspiring. 'Lovely day!' he said.

'I thought you weren't coming.' The old woman fetched from a blue-painted tin on the mantelpiece some dollar notes and her rent book.

'How's your husband?' he asked, pressing the rent book against the door jamb and writing in it.

She placed the notes in his hand and turned her head aside. 'Much the same.'

'No word yet of the operation?' He closed the book, returned it and folded the notes into his wallet. His half-hidden eyes appeared for a moment and furtively swept the length of the weedy vegetable garden. 'The fact is, there's something I've been wanting to say to you. I put it off on account of your husband being in hospital. But the weeks are running on. This place is to be sold.'

She stared past him, her face stony and expressionless. 'Have you forgotten what you said when we came into it – that you were not going to sell it?' she asked.

'I haven't forgotten. But it would cost me over eight hundred dollars to paint it. The rates are eighty dollars a quarter. There's tax on the rent ... insurance ...'

She continued to stare past him, as though not listening. He raised his voice. 'You pay a very low rent.'

'But you said –' She faltered. 'You said if we did it up ourselves inside … We bought the paint, the wallpaper. We painted it ourselves.'

'It doesn't pay me to keep it.'

'There was no garden,' she said. 'My husband made the garden. It's everything to him.'

He looked at her shrewdly. 'Would you be interested in buying the house yourself?'

Her eyes lit up as though a sudden prospect opened out before her. The next moment her face clouded over. 'I'll look for another place,' she said.

He made a movement as though he would shake hands, but she did not see.

'I have to catch the early bus to get a seat in the hospital lobby,' she said.

'Explain to your husband how it is,' he said, rubbing one of his hands over the back of the other.

In her bedroom she sat on the side of her big old double bed and changed into a pair of shoes. She took off her apron, put on a black cardigan and black straw hat with a large bow, took up gloves, handbag, walking stick, and going back to the sink lifted the gladioli from the bucket of water and wrapped them in a sheet of brown paper. Looking briefly round the kitchen, she went out the back door, locked it, and dropped the large iron key into her handbag.

The hospital lobby was deserted. A few worn chairs stood against a bare wall. The old woman sat down with a sigh and placed her bunch of gladioli on the floor, hung her walking stick on the arm of the chair and folded her gloved hands over her handbag on her knee.

A heavily built nurse with thick legs fastened a rope across the corridor. 'Visiting hour is not till two,' she said.

The old woman looked at the clock above the reception desk. It was ten past one.

'I come early to get a seat,' she said, bowing her head.
She was alone for a long time. Gradually the lobby filled
with people carrying flowers, baskets, paper bags. A din of
voices rose around her. The air became hot and heavy with
the scent of flowers and women's perfume. A porter came
and fastened back the outside doors to let in more air. But
none of this the old woman noticed. She sat slumped in her
chair, her hands in her lap, her head sunk in her shoulders.
She looked up only when the porter unhooked the rope that
had closed the corridor.

The old man's bed was at the end of a large ward. He did
not see her come in, limping, heavy, bent low over her stick.
His eyes were closed. The pillows and sheets looked smooth,
and he, too, looked pale and clean as though his face had
been scrubbed. His hands, lying on the white sheets, were
knotted like old roots.

The old woman laid one of her own hands over his and
woke him. A pair of dark eyes appeared in the pale scrubbed
face and their gaze fell on the sheaf of gladioli. 'Y' didn't cut
'em, did y'?'

She placed the flowers on the bed and drew up a stool.

'Ah, it's wasted, bringin' 'em in here,' the old man said.
'They don't know how to look after 'em. They won't leave
'em in the ward. You'll see. When y' come tomorrow they'll
be gawn.'

'There's more coming on.'

'I been thinkin' of them bean shaws – have y' burnt 'em
yet?'

'The beans are finished.'

'I know they're finished. Y' can't leave 'em there. They
had the rust this year. We'll have it next year. They gotta be
burnt, I tell y'!'

The old woman sighed and gazed at the bed next to his,
which was empty. A light overcoat lay across the foot of it.

The old man looked at her vindictively. 'Y'll have to thin the onions or they'll be no use.'

'It's seems such a waste to pull them out ...'

'Waste? Aaah! I know you! Y' let 'em push each other in the rows. I'll never come out of this!'

The old woman's stone face turned towards him. 'You make up your mind to come through it all right and you will.'

'I'm eighty-seven,' he whimpered. 'That spiritualist woman we went to see that time – she told me I'd die at eighty-seven!'

The old woman took one of the gnarled hands between her own.

'You stop fretting. The garden's all right. There's more cabbages than I know what to do with – and such a size you never saw.'

'Don't leave 'em there – eating all the good out of the ground! Give 'em away.' He closed his eyes and a tear ran down his cheek. He rubbed it away with the back of his free hand. He was silent so long he appeared to have fallen asleep. Suddenly, without opening his eyes, he said, 'The operation's tomorrow.'

A young man with straight blond hair came to the foot of the bed.

'Well, I'm off home, Pop.' He picked up the overcoat from the empty bed.

The old man looked up. 'You reckon I'll come out of this, Jack?'

'At the rate you're going, you'll live to be a hundred, Pop,' the young man said.

'I hope you get on all right, Jack,' the old man said.

'I'll get on all right. Don't you worry. That's a nice red gladdy you got there.'

The old man unwrapped the brown paper from the gladioli and held up the single red bloom.

'Cockscomb. I gave fifty cents for that bulb.' He turned the heavy flower till it caught the light from the window. The petals were trembling.

'It's a beaut,' the young man said.

'If y' ever grow them make sure they get plenty water.' He began to look at the other blooms and the young man waved goodbye and left.

One by one he held them up to the light and examined them, the pink, apricot, white and the scarlet.

'There's a yeller one to come out,' he said to the old woman. 'I wouldn't mind seeing that one.'

'I'll watch for it,' the old woman said.

'You giving 'em water?'

'I can't be carrying buckets of water down there.'

A fierce light burned in his eyes. 'Y'd let 'em die, y' would!'

'The tap runs so slow ...' she said.

'Y'll have to tell old Bloodpressure the pipes are done. He'll have to put in new pipes. When does he come for the rent?'

'He came today. He had on a straw hat. It's very hot out.'

'Did y' have the money?'

'Yes.'

'What's he got to say?'

The old woman looked round the ward, at the other visitors, the other patients, the fawn blind that had been drawn down over an open window by the empty bed and was being slowly sucked out and in by a current of air.

'Nothing. He's got nothing to say.'

'You tell him about the pipes next time.'

'He asked how you were.'

The old man seemed pleased. He closed his eyes and smiled to himself. In a few moments his hands relaxed their grip on the flower stems. His mouth sagged open. He was asleep.

A nurse came to the next bed, drew the curtains round it and brought in a new patient, a stout, middle-aged man in a dark-red dressing gown. The visitors' bell rang, and the visitors beside the other beds began to drift away.

The old woman sat on, not noticing.

At the Port

Amy's mother did not go to work on Saturdays. She wore shorts and a cotton shirt, and if she intended to go out at night, washed her hair and set it in curlers. On weekdays she wore a long black skirt and black pointed shoes with high heels and kept her hair very neat and smooth because she was a salesperson in the mantles at Smart's in town. She was quite small, not as big as some of the schoolgirls Amy saw getting off the bus when she went to meet her.

Everybody called her Marge, even Amy. But Mr Longwell, the painter who painted Gran's house, called her Noddy. Sometimes he stopped Amy in the street and asked, 'How's Noddy? Tell her I was asking after her.'

Gran, whose house they lived in, was quite different, large and fat, and she swayed as she walked, making the measuring-tape, which she wore round her neck, sway from side to side. But she did not walk far, she stayed at home all day, sewing on her machine, or pressing with her steam-iron, making children's clothes for a children's-wear shop in town. In her front sitting room there were big windows that looked out over the water to the hills on the other side of the harbour. In the centre of the room stood a steel rack on wheels where she hung the finished clothes waiting for Mrs Macnamara to call and collect them. Mrs Macnamara, who wore big glasses and earrings like ice-cubes, pulled the clothes roughly backwards and forwards and held them up to look at them, though Amy was not allowed to even touch them. 'Your hands will make them dirty,' Gran told her. And Amy didn't touch them because the big photo of Grandad above the fireplace was always watching. The front bedroom that looked out on the harbour was Gran's, too. Everything belonged to Gran. Marge was always saying, 'Be careful with that, don't forget it's Gran's', or 'Don't sit in Gran's chair', or 'Not in Gran's house, please.' But Amy liked Gran, even if she was too busy sometimes to look up from her work.

One Saturday, when it was very hot and both the front door and back door stood open all day, 'To catch a breeze from the harbour', Gran said, Marge tied a red scarf round the curlers in her hair and went to the corner store for some groceries, bringing back an orange drink for Amy and a newspaper for Gran. Amy sat at the kitchen table sucking her drink and making an interesting noise with her straw while Marge packed away the groceries and Gran opened the newspaper and put on her reading glasses.

'Marge!' Gran exclaimed suddenly, 'Alf Longwell, the painter who lives along the main road and who painted the house, has had an accident at the wharves and is drowned!'

'What?' Marge was opening the fridge door and held a carton of eggs in one hand. She turned suddenly and the open door knocked the eggs to the floor. Her face changed to a deep red colour like sunburn. But she hardly seemed to notice what had happened to the eggs, even though Amy said, 'Oooh, you broke the eggs!' Gran, too, took no notice.

'It's here, in the paper,' she said.

Marge knelt on the floor, picked up the eggs that were not broken and after wiping up the others moved to the bench and looked out of the window leaning on her hands with her back to the room. Even her neck had turned red.

'I saw Mrs Longwell only the other day,' Gran said. 'She was going past with the two children. The baby is still in the pram. I feel for her. I shall never forget the day I heard that your father was drowned. It was a hot day just like this – I had brought in the washing from the line and I was folding it on this table. The policeman came to the open door and walked in. I saw his face. My mouth turned so dry I couldn't speak. My whole world was turned upside down. So it will be for Mrs Longwell.'

'But here, at the wharves,' Marge said in a low voice without turning round.

'I didn't want your father to go down to Campbell Island in that small boat,' Gran said. She took off her glasses and brushed a tear from her cheek.

'You wonder how it could happen,' Marge said in a whisper.

Amy, too, wondered how it could happen. 'Why didn't Mr Longwell swim?' she asked.

'We must call and see her,' Gran said.

'Take your drink outside,' Marge said, still speaking in a strange low voice and continuing to lean on the bench and look out of the window, though there was nothing to be seen out there but the wall of the wash-house.

'I've finished.' Amy knew they wanted to get rid of her. They never explained anything. 'It's too hot outside.'

'It's cooler now,' Gran said, looking at her as though she had just remembered she was there. 'You could play in the shade.'

'I don't want to.'

They took no further notice of her. Gran unfolded a clean handkerchief, wiped her glasses and put them on again. Amy wanted to hear more about Mr Longwell. She knew about Grandad, but that was before she was born. It was very quiet in the room. All she could hear was the rustle of Gran's paper and the murmur of the waves on the gravel beach below the cliff, with a few seagulls crying as they passed overhead. She decided to go out and see if there was anyone in the street.

She went out through the open front door and crunched circles on the path of broken oyster shells that Grandad had made before he was drowned. She couldn't swing on the gate because it had one broken hinge and hung open sideways. Grandad would have mended it if he had been here, Gran said, but he was not here. Mona Greenfellow's grandad had mended her gate and Mona had a father, too, and Amy wished she had a father, but had never had one, not even one that was drowned like Grandad and Mr Longwell. But the gate with one broken hinge made a sort of ladder, so she climbed up to the corner post where she could see part of the harbour and looked up and down the street. The setting sun shone into her eyes, but she could see the big ship that was tied up at the wharves looming high above the roofs of the houses.

She liked Mr Longwell. He had a black beard and very bright eyes. One day when she was in town with Marge he gave them a ride back to the port. The step into his van was too high for Marge to climb up in her narrow black skirt. Mr Longwell laughed and pushed her up by her bottom and made her squeal. He wanted to help Amy, too, but she climbed up by herself. When Mr Longwell got into the cab on the other side he put his arm round Marge and said he was sorry he hurt her and gave her a long kiss. He asked her if she liked his beard, and she said a kiss without whiskers was like an egg without salt, and he laughed a lot and kissed her again and said, 'That's my own Noddy', and they had fun all the way home.

Now he was drowned, Gran said, and everyone would be down at the wharves to see how it had happened. There was nobody passing in the street. The air was warm and there was a strong smell of seaweed. The people would be standing around like the day two cars banged together at the corner. She would go and see for herself. It didn't matter that she was not allowed to go down to the wharves. They wouldn't miss her.

She climbed down. Outside Mr Longwell's house she saw four strange cars. His van was parked in the drive at the side of the house. The curtains in the front windows were pulled across as though it was night already. In the side street she saw Kerby Longwell jumping backwards and forwards over the ditch and singing.

'What are you doing?' she asked.

Kerby smiled and said, 'Hi!'

'You were jumping over the ditch and singing,' she said. 'I saw you.'

Kerby stood on one foot and dragged the other round him in the dust of the road. 'I wasn't doing nothing,' he said.

'Your father's drowned,' Amy said sternly, stiffening her back in imitation of Gran. 'You're not supposed to jump and sing.' She remembered something Gran said and added, 'I am not impressed.' She didn't know what the word meant, but tried it.

Kerby walked backwards into his father's grassy drive, then turned and ran round the house out of sight.

Down at the wharves an engine towing a few trucks was moving so slowly along the railway lines that there was just time to cross. She wondered what would happen if she tripped and fell. Would the engine driver see her and stop the train in time? Perhaps it would stop at the very last moment? That would scare everyone. That would make them sorry they had sent her outside. She ran to the edge of the wharves and looked over. The water was a long way down, green, and making a licking sound against the black piles. Brown ropes of seaweed moved when the water moved. There were no people standing around. At the other end of the wharves, away past the big ship that was in, she could see some men with a truck who had come down to collect fish from one of the boats that were moored there. She decided to go and watch them.

Going past the big ship, she saw two men up on the deck shouting at each other and waving their arms, and she waited to see if there was going to be a fight, but they moved back out of sight. Nothing else to see. No people. When she was clear of the ship, she found a space where she could crouch down at the edge and look into the water again. If you fell down there you could hang on to the ropes of seaweed and keep floating till someone came along in a boat. The water was deep, but it was calm. The seaweed had roots like trees and grew on the piles.

Suddenly she felt her arm grabbed by someone who pulled her roughly back from the edge. She lost her balance and stumbled. Her face came close to two bare legs in red sandals.

'What are you doing down here?' Marge was standing over her, gripping her arm so tightly it hurt. She was breathing hard and said in a temper, 'You little horror', and shook her. 'Do you want another tragedy? I can't cope with the pain I've got already.'

She released Amy and began to cry, standing quite still and making no sound, but with trembling lips and tears running down her cheeks. She touched them with a screwed up handkerchief and said quietly, 'Come home.'

Amy followed miserably as they began to walk back. Marge walked slowly, but Amy lagged behind, fearing she was going to be punished. She had never been allowed to go down to the wharves on her own. Marge must have run all the way in her shorts and shirt, without even tying a scarf around her curlers, as she did when she went to the grocer's shop; she walked past Mr Longwell's house without looking up, but Amy stopped and stared. She saw more cars parked there and people walking up the front path carrying flowers and plates of food.

'Marge,' she called, running to catch up with her. 'Did you see the flowers and cakes?' she asked excitedly. 'Kerby Longwell is going to have a party!'

Her mother walked on without answering.

'Marge!' Amy tugged her mother's shirt. 'Why haven't I got a father?'